choose**life**

A national strategy and action plan
to prevent suicide in Scotland

Sponsorship for this project was obtained from Choose Life,
the national suicide prevention programme for Scotland.

Children and young people are a target group for Choose Life
and substance misuse is a risk factor for suicide and self harm.

To find out more about local and national
Choose Life initiatives you can visit: **www.chooselife.net**

A Glenmill Publication

First published in 2006

Glenmill Publishing

Dumfries

Scotland

DG2 8PX

tel: 01387 270 861

www.first-base.org

British Library Cataloguing in Publication Data.
A catalogue record of this book
is available from the British Library.

ISBN 0 9551057 1 4

Glenmill logo: Andrew Carroll AKA 'Gizmo'

Printed and bound in Great Britain

ChildLine Scotland

0800 1111

ChildLine is the free helpline for children and young people in distress. It provides a confidential telephone counselling service for any young person with any problem, 24 hours a day, every day. It listens, comforts and protects. Trained volunteer counsellors provide support and advice, and can refer young people to appropriate helping agencies, if this is what the young person wants.

Sometimes the problems experienced by children and young people are so painful that they consider suicide as a means of ending the pain. If a young person feels there is nothing left to look forward to and feels completely alone ChildLine listens, and helps to reduce feelings of isolation and despair.

If you are feeling suicidal please talk to someone – parents, friends or trusted adults. If you don't want to talk to someone you know you can phone ChildLine on freephone 0800 1111 or write to Freepost 1111, Glasgow, G1 1BR.

If it feels like there is no one to turn to, no one to remove the pain or simply to just listen to you, ChildLine will be there for you.

About the Book

The First Base Agency is a small charity based in Dumfries. We are a drug, alcohol and gambling information, advice and support centre. We support families affected by the substance misuse of a son or daughter or grandchild or husband or wife. Almost every day parents bring in sons and daughters who are slowly but surely destroying their lives with a variety of drugs. Many of these young people have taken the Road to Down and reached the place where nothing seems worth living for any more: the place where the sanctuary of suicide seems preferable to the grinding misery of carrying on with life. Several of these young people are only with us today due to the absolute excellence of the Dumfries and Galloway emergency services.

This book is funded by the 'Choose Life' initiative which supports projects which try to make an impact on the national suicide rate. The headlines say that we are the fourth richest country on planet earth. We have an abundance of food, unprecedented opportunities and, thanks to our grandparents who slammed the door in Hitler's face, the freedom to vote for who we like and say what we think. No generation has had more going for it and yet no generation has ever been so depressed. 'Roads to Down' is about how drugs play a part in sending so many young lives into darkness. The stories don't come from New York or London or Amsterdam. They come from here. Scotland 2005. The characters are made up, but what happens is only too real.

Life is all about Choices. Read 'Roads to Down' and you'll find out a little about the stuff that the global drugs industry likes to keep under wraps. Check out the downside. And then if you choose to spend your cash on these products, at least do so with your eyes open. We see too many young people who have sleepwalked into a life of utter misery without really having a clue of the risks they are taking.

Mark Frankland
Education Manager
The First Base Agency
6 Buccleuch St
Dumfries

mark@thecull.com
01387 279 680

DO YOU WANT TO BUY COPIES OF THIS BOOK?

'Roads to Down' is available free of charge
throughout Dumfries and Galloway
thanks to funding from the 'Choose Life' initiative.

Outside of Dumfries and Galloway,
copies are available at the following prices.

1 - 9 Copies:	**£1.75**
10 – 99 Copies:	**£1.50**
100 – 999 Copies:	**£1.25**
1000 + Copies:	**£1.00**

To place an order please call

01387 279 680

or log on to **www.first-base.org**

or complete the **order form** at the back of the book

Contents

CHAPTER ONE   Page   1
Bella

CHAPTER TWO   Page   29
Stevo

CHAPTER THREE   Page   61
Chelle

Chapter One

Bella

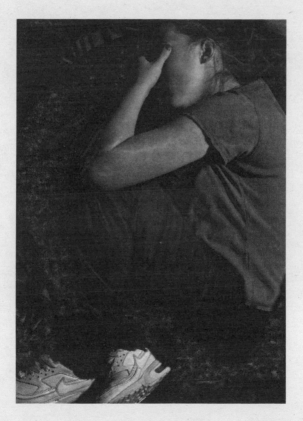

Introduction

A SPOTLIGHT ON CANNABIS: A FIRST BASE
AGENCY ARTICLE FROM THE DUMFRIES STANDARD, 2005

We can learn a lot about the way that society has come to feel about cannabis smoking from the way it is often presented to us. Take the case of T-shirts. It is a common sight on the High Street to see people of both sexes and most ages marching happily along in a T-shirt with a cannabis leaf on the front. Why? What message are they trying to give out about themselves? And what message are we expected to receive? Ever since Woodstock and Dylan and the long hair version Beatles, cannabis has had a Peace and Love and flower power image to it. The person in the T-shirt is saying look at me, I smoke dope which makes it pretty unlikely that I have a Stanley knife on me and I'm not the sort of guy to get in your face and scream "What d'yu think you're looking at pal?" with beery breath. Instead the image is one of a laid-back, thoughtful person who might well watch films with subtitles.

These T-shirts emphasise the fact that cannabis is a plant that has been grown for thousands of years and is very much a part of nature. Fair enough. And yet few other substances seem to able to make this link and get away with it. We see people in Jack Daniels and Budweiser T-shirts, but I am yet to see anyone with a picture of some ears of barley emblazoned over their chest. Similarly if our local heroin users took to the High Street in T-shirts with pictures of nice colourful Afghan poppies I don't think it would be all that well received by the public at large. Maybe the poppy is after all a more wicked type of flora than the cannabis leaf.

3

If it is not a cannabis leaf that is on display, it is often a burning joint. Again the message is meant to be fairly cosy; the wearer of this T-shirt likes to smoke an illegal substance but that only goes to show he has a heart of gold. Again a picture of a needle poised over a vein or a nose hovering over a line of coke would not be T-shirt acceptable.

Of course the reason why dope smokers wear leaf pictures whilst lager drinkers wouldn't dream of adorning themselves in grain images is easy to find. Drinking lager is perfectly legal so long as you are over eighteen, which means that the drink itself isn't remotely cool. It is the label that can be cool which is why the drinks industry spends endless millions on trying to make their brands give out the right messages. There are no cannabis brands. Only the plant itself, so when the cannabis smoker wears the T-shirt, their message is that yes, I may not carry a knife but I'm not boring because I break the law on a regular basis.

Is this relevant? Scotland and Holland, compare and contrast. Both are North European countries with a population of about five million. In Holland, once you reach a certain age it is OK to go into a cannabis café and choose your dope from a menu. In Scotland dope smoking is illegal even if you are a hundred years old. The result? In Holland, 5% of the 15 to 30 age group regularly smoke cannabis. In Scotland the figure is double that. 10%. So the place where it is illegal under all circumstances has twice the number of regular smokers. Why? Maybe it is only the fact that cannabis is illegal that makes it cool. Dutch youngsters look through the doors of a cannabis café and see people like their parents inside. Nothing cool about that. I don't suppose you would make much of a fortune peddling cannabis T-shirts in Amsterdam.

The way we see dope smoking on television is also interesting. Those shown having a joint are generally characterised as mildly goofy figures, but good old boys at heart. It isn't all that different to the way that drunk people are portrayed. Somebody who is falling down drunk is fair game for comedy. Similarly, someone who is stoned and giggling is often seen as amusing. And yet when we see the needle being pressed home or the cocaine going up the nose it needs to be well after the watershed and we are warned that we are about to watch 'scenes of drug use'. The unmistakable conclusion that many young people draw from all of this is that cannabis really is pretty well OK and that is why the government has finally seen sense and downgraded it from a Class B drug to Class C. Surely over the next few years they will at last see sense and make it legal alongside the other legally available drugs, alcohol and tobacco.

On the surface, the arguments in favour of cannabis being acceptable are quite compelling, especially when it is compared with fags and booze. Here are the bare bones. Cigarettes. Smoked by fifteen million Brits. Fiercely addictive. Responsible for 100,000 deaths per year. Alcohol. Used by over fifty million Brits. Fiercely addictive. Responsible for 30,000 deaths a year and 75% of all violent crime. Cannabis. Used by between five and fifteen million Brits. Non-addictive. Responsible for no deaths per year. No link with violence. On the basis of this information, many feel that any sane Government would rush to legalise cannabis and ban booze and fags. In 2000 the Eindhoven Council was facing a rough couple of days. The small Dutch town was battening down the hatches and bracing itself for an invasion of thirty thousand English football fans and they feared it would be like a human version of hurricane Katrina. They dealt with the threat by offering short term licences for many of the town's bars to sell cannabis and the visiting fans all got well and truly stoned and went round hugging the locals rather than head butting them. The Council were so pleased with the result that they passed the information to the Council of the small Belgian town, Charlerloi, which was the next port of call for the travelling fans. The Belgians took no heed of the advice and the fans got drunk instead of stoned and the town was duly smashed to pieces. When we watch pictures of our Saturday night town centres on the TV, it is hard not to have some appreciation of the Eindhoven solution. The UN has recently voted Scotland the most violent country in the developed world and that is not a result of cannabis smoking.

I can sense that many reading this must now be getting hot under the collar and about to toss the paper across the room in anger. Are these First Base people using this space to extol the virtues of the weed?

Actually, we're not.

Honest.

The first part of this article has been an attempt to show just how much confusion now surrounds the whole issue of cannabis. On the one hand the Government says it really might not be so bad after all so we will downgrade it. On the other hand the police still have the power to lock us up for a decent period of time if they catch us with a lump in our pocket. In the middle of all this, it gets pretty difficult for parents in particular to know where to start when it comes to talking to our children. If we start to tell them things that are completely untrue they will simply switch off. This is where we tend to go wrong. If we say something along the lines of 'if you smoke cannabis you will get addicted and die' they will immediately switch off on us completely because they know full well that it simply isn't true. That is why it is important to talk in facts and not in myths and media hype. So here are a few facts which when added together make not smoking cannabis seem a pretty good idea.

1: The legal stuff. It is important to remember that all the news stories about it being OK to smoke a joint refer to England NOT Scotland. Being picked up with a lump of cannabis in your pocket in Dumfries means something very different to having the same thing happen in Carlisle. The police line here is very simple. If you get caught the cannabis will be confiscated, you will be charged, and the matter will be referred to the Procurator Fiscal. If the issue goes all the way to the Sheriff you will end up with a record for being caught in possession of drugs. With the best will in the world, this isn't the best thing to have on your CV. If you're expecting a copper to give you an avuncular wink and send you on your way, well don't hold your breath.

2: Exams. Even the most ardent cannabis fan wouldn't try to claim that smoking dope makes the brain work like a Rolls Royce. Basically cannabis and exams mix about as happily as Celtic and Rangers fans. You might have read about the school down in Kent where they have introduced random drugs testing amidst a blaze of publicity. The trial has now been running for a year and some results are starting to emerge. Last year, before the testing, 22% of pupils achieved five good GSEs or better. This year the figure has risen to over 40%. Same school, same teachers, same subjects. The difference? Cannabis stays in the system for up to thirty-five days so it looks like the kids in Kent decided to play it safe and stop the joints.

3: Avoiding brain damage. This is a secret that at last seems to be making its way out from under the carpet. For thousands of years human beings have smoked the cannabis plant without doing any great harm to ourselves. In fact these are the kinds of varieties that many would now like to see licensed for medicinal use. The problem we now face is that many of the varieties of cannabis bear no relationship to the stuff that Dylan and the Beatles took on board. Like many other plants, cannabis has fallen into the hands of the scientists who have done their stuff and genetically modified new superstrength varieties that are generally called 'skunk'. People smoke cannabis to alter their brains into a different shape where things seem funny and food tastes great. Skunk alters the brain a whole lot more than the regulation product which is why it commands a premium. Unfortunately we are now finding that skunk can alter a young brain all the way to psychosis and schizophrenia. Since the drug was reclassified a couple of years ago in England, we have seen cannabis related admissions to psychiatric units quadruple. I'll say that again. Quadruple. As in scary, scary. Research into this new phenomenon is in its infancy, but it appears that the developing brains of adolescents are horribly vulnerable to skunk. Think of a tree. If you have a swing at a hundred-year-old oak tree with an axe, you really won't do it much harm. But if you clobber the same tree when it is just a year old sapling you will probably kill it. The growing number of young people who now have serious mental health problems as a result of smoking skunk is a new nightmare that we will all come to know more and more about over the next few years.

4: Depression. It is important to remember that what cannabis does is enhance the way you already feel. So a mildly amusing joke suddenly becomes the funniest thing you've ever heard. A banana milkshake, which normally tastes pretty good, suddenly seems as if it has been beamed straight down from somewhere in heaven. What people forget to mention is that this swings both ways. So if you are feeling a bit down and you decide a joint might make the world a brighter place, then think again. All it will do is change feeling a bit gloomy into full on depression and the more you smoke the worse it will get. We see a lot of depressed youngsters who keep trying to smoke themselves happy and only make it worse.

5: The 'gateway drug'. Start smoking cannabis and you'll end up on heroin. We hear a lot of this and there is barely a shred of evidence to back it up. In Holland where smoking cannabis is acceptable they have about 8,000 heroin addicts. We have 65,000. A pretty compelling statistic. However there is plenty of evidence that shows that smoking cannabis is indeed a gateway to the number one killer drug of them all. Lots of young people successfully stay clear of smoking cigarettes. Then they start smoking joints and find that they need more and more. It takes a while for the penny to drop. It isn't the cannabis their body is craving. It is the nicotine which of course IS very addictive. So they start buying cigarettes instead.

Hopefully these are five reasons for youngsters to think long and hard before saying yes to a joint. Permanent brain damage really isn't very cool no matter how you try to dress it up. Skunk is very, very dangerous and the sooner we all wake up to the fact, the better..

Bella
Part One: Winter

A clock. And a mirror. And a decision. And Bella's mind ran like a freaked rabbit between the three. The clock said ten past eight and her dad had already called up the stairs twice. It didn't really matter what time she arrived at the party, but he was going to drop her off on his way to snooker and there was now an edge of annoyance in his voice.

The mirror. The mirror that never gave the answers she wanted. Bella was under no illusion as to what answer she wanted from the mirror. There was not a single fifteen-year-old girl on planet earth who was in any doubt as to what was expected from the mirror. The answer was in her face every time she helped her mum out with the weekly shop at Tesco. The minute she walked through the main door, her eyes were drawn to line upon line of magazines where the scantily clad figures on the covers weighed in at an average of about six stones each – dripping wet. It was what Bella had aspired to for as long as she could remember. She felt as if she had been starving herself from the moment her legs had woken up to the fact that they were for walking. The starvation process had escalated for the last three weeks following confirmation that she had indeed been invited to the undisputed event of the year: Jennifer Bentley's fifteenth birthday party.

She couldn't escape the fact that her total joy at being invited to the party was somewhat ridiculous as Jennifer Bentley was without doubt the human being she hated more than any other in the whole wide world. Jenny would have looked quite at home on the cover of any of the ranks of magazines in Tesco and my god didn't she know it. She flaunted her way around the school attracting a constant stream of comment from every boy who laid eyes on her. Bella would probably have loathed Jennifer Bentley had she been a deaf mute. She would have loathed her for the very simple fact of her stomach. Jennifer Bentley's stomach was a thing that was on constant display. Winter or summer, rain or shine she would manipulate her clothing to ensure that the flattest stomach in Dumfries and Galloway was on constant display. Just like the ones on the covers of the Tesco magazines. If you were to give Jenny's belly a spray of green paint it would have made a more than adequate snooker table and there would never have been any shortage of drooling lads ready to put down their fifty pence pieces for a game.

The stomach that stared back from the mirror bore about as much resemblance to the Bentley belly as a stray cat with an ear missing next to a Bengal tiger. The three-week hunger strike seemed to have made no difference whatsoever. As far as Bella was concerned, the stomach that stared back at her was a grotesquely enormous swelling of chalk white flab. Of course Jennifer Bentley's mum had a sun bed in one of the spare rooms which meant that Jennifer Bentley's belly was never anything but a rich brown. Bella had nagged her mum to give her some money to go to one of the tanning studios in the town only to be told not to be so silly.

So, yes. A deaf and dumb Jennifer would have been a figure of hate. But Jennifer wasn't deaf and dumb. Anything but. She was the proud owner of a tongue that could cut through any defence like a diamond-tipped drill bit. Every day she marched the school corridors with her small gang of followers, spitting poison at all around her. And in Jenny's book a few extra pounds was reason enough to make one of her half heard comments that would send her disciples into fits of giggles. They were the skinny Mafia. Short skirts and highlighted hair and well-practised smirking faces that showed constant contempt for those around them who fought a losing battle against their puppy fat. Puppy fat. These were two words that were like curdled milk in Bella's ears. Her mum's words. No need to worry hen. It's just natural. It will go away. Just you wait and see.

Well right now the mirror was telling her in no uncertain terms that it hadn't gone away. Instead it had got worse. The sight of her non-magazine belly brought a prickling of tears into her eyes. She had invested six weeks worth of hard saved pocket money on the crop top for the party and all it showed was a sickening expanse of blubber.

"Come on Bella for God's sake, it's nearly twenty past!"

Her dad's words forced the decision ever nearer. Option one. Wear the new top and risk the contemptuous laughter of the skinny Mafia as they laid mocking eyes on her flab. Option two. Wear a baggy T-shirt and be mocked for being a skaff. Two weeks of under five hundred calories per day, and nothing. Damn. She wrenched off the top and hurled it across the room and pulled on the T-shirt. Better a skaff than a whale. For a moment she wondered whether the best thing would be to act sick and not go at all. But she had looked forward to the party for ages. She hesitated for a few more seconds then took the plunge and went downstairs.

The Bentleys lived in a big house a couple of miles out of the town. A stream of cars dropped off the party guests.

"Behave yourself then."

Her dad gave her an encouraging smile which made her feel sixty times worse than she was feeling already, and that was bad enough. Party time. Yeah right. In front of her one of the senior members of the skinny Mafia was ringing the bell. The door swung open to reveal Jennifer Bentley celebrating entering her sixteenth year by wearing an outfit that was as near as possible to the one she had worn as she had popped out into the world. Her crop top barely made it below her breasts and her skirt was of 'the hardly covers the knickers' variety. She wrapped her fellow member of the thin club in an exaggerated embrace before giving Bella a look of mild amusement.

"Hi Bella. Come on in."

At least she wasn't early. The place was already full and the music was loud in her ears. There were plenty of the puppy-fat brigade who had thrown caution to the wind and gone for the crop tops. Bella didn't really know what to think. None of them seemed all that bothered at showing off their less than Bentleyesque stomachs. In fact they seemed sickeningly at ease and the fact that two or three were already being ferociously snogged suggested that the lads were not over concerned at their non-snooker table bellies.

"Why aren't you wearing that new top then?"

She hadn't noticed her best friend Ellie come over. They had been out and chosen their party gear together a couple of Saturdays earlier.

Ellie was a fully paid up member of the puppy-fat brigade and obviously had no qualms at putting it on public view.

"Changed my mind. I couldn't be bothered with Mum telling me I looked like a jumped-up tart."

Ellie took her to where she had stashed a bag full of alco-pops that she had persuaded her older brother to buy in return for a commission of two bottles for himself. After a couple of fast-guzzled bottles, Bella was feeling about eighty times better about life. They were dancing now along with Tina, third member of their group.

"Fancy going out for a bit?" Tina had to shout to be heard over the beat.

"You joking! It's freezing."

"Come on. I've got a surprise.."

It was freezing. A sky full of stars glittered over the Bentleys' manicured garden. As soon as they stepped out the cold hit them and covered them in goose bumps.

"You HAVE to be joking Tina . . . " Ellie was not at all taken with the glories of a crisp winter night and was ready for going back in.

"Wait a second. Here. Look." With an air of great triumph she pulled an expertly rolled joint from her tiny handbag. "I made our Neil roll it for me. He says it's top gear. It better had be. He charged me three quid the robbing sod."

She pulled out a lighter and soon had the joint glowing bright orange in the dark of the night. Bella had been cold enough when the night air had wrapped itself around her sweating limbs. Now she was a lump of ice. The moment had arrived like a supersonic jet flying low over the Galloway hills. No warning. She had never taken drugs and she had always told herself that she never would. The High Street was a living advert for not doing so. No way was she ever going to end up like the pinched-faced skeletons who flitted in and out of the shops with burning hunger in their eyes. But this was not how it was supposed to be. It was supposed to be a stranger. A hard-faced guy in a hoodie making her an offer that she could easily refuse. Not this. Not Ellie and Tina. Her friends. Her two best friends. Her allies against the mocking sneers of the skinny Mafia. And now the joint was offered to Ellie and Ellie was taking it and smoking it in a way that said that it wasn't the first time.

"Here you are Bella."

She shook her head. Mouth dry. Stomach churning. A vision of her dad's kind eyes in the car. "No. You're all right . . . "

"Don't be so soft. Come on. Have a go. It's only a bit of dope."

"No honestly. I'm fine. I really am."

"Course you are. And this'll make you a whole lot finer. Come on. Don't be so boring."

Bella hung her head. "I don't know how."

"It's easy. Look . . . " Ellie sucked in a lungful of smoke, held for a few seconds, then exhaled. "Just don't take too much OK. Just a bit. Take it in, hold it, breathe it out . . . Go on . . . just try it . . . "

The first go was a complete disaster and ended with a racking bout of coughing that amused the others no end. The second attempt was better. She managed to hold back the coughing long enough for the cannabis to make it up into her brain and announce itself. The third attempt was achieved without any coughing at all. As the joint moved on back to Tina, Bella was aware that the back of her throat was on its way up to the top of her skull and the music seemed to be pouring out through the open window above her and down into her ears like warm honey. Two more draws and Tina dragged the last bit of life out of the joint. For a moment the three of them stared at each other, not at all concerned now with the chill of the night. Ellie's eyes were drawn to a drain a couple of yards from where they stood and her shoulders started to shake with laughter.

"What?"

Ellie pointed at the drain and found it hard to pick words out of her growing hysterics.

"That . . . the drain . . . I bet Mr Bentley had to order it specially . . . He couldn't have anything with big gaps . . . because . . . because . . . because Jenny might fall through it . . . "

When Bella thought about it later she was struck by the fact that it really wasn't all that funny at all. Not in hindsight. But at the time it was the funniest thing she had ever heard and the laughter that took her seemed to turn every bone in her body into rubber. The more they laughed, the worse it got until they had tears pouring down their cheeks, and ribs that ached.

It took a good five minutes before they felt capable of going back inside. As soon as they stepped into the living room they were confronted by the sight of the tanned angular form of Jennifer Bentley dancing to the growling words of 50 Cent and in that very instant the same image leapt into their brains. A giant drain and the skinny form of Jennifer Bentley falling through the gap and once again the laughter took them and soon everyone in the room was watching them and that only made it worse. And there was a new look in the eyes of Jennifer Bentley. It was a look Bella had never seen before. Doubt. Because Jennifer Bentley had sensed that the three members of the fat club were actually laughing at her. And Bella without doubt felt better than she had ever felt in her whole life. Ever.

Part Two
Spring

The warm evening sun leaked in through the open window and lay across Bella's face like a sleepy cat. The easing sound of Goldfrapp slid out of her Ipod and into her brain making her thoughts blur and swim. She put her face close to the open air and blew out a plume of smoke having held the long draw on her joint for as long as she could. Outside she could see their neighbour's young children having their first go of the year in their extra-large paddling pool. Had she not been wearing headphones she would have been able to hear their excited shouts along with the soft hum of bees. The joint had a last pull left in it and she duly sucked it down before stubbing it out on the window ledge and folding what was left into a piece of paper before throwing the tight package into the bin.

Her eyes were drawn to the text books which were waiting hopefully on her desk. Bella stared at the books and the books seemed to stare back with an air of resentment. According to the rather hopeful revision timetable she had written out a few weeks earlier, these books should have been filed away to the memory banks at least a fortnight earlier. The timetable was now broken beyond repair. The truth was that even if she had stuck to it religiously she would have still arrived at the day of her first exam too far behind.

When she allowed herself to think about it she knew that her studies had gone to rack and ruin over the last six months. For a decade Bella had always hovered near the top of every class she had been a part of. She had never been one of those who had been in bother for not doing homework. She was a naturally organised person and it had never been a problem to keep up with the demands of schoolwork. At least it hadn't been. The problem was that it was a very different Bella who now closed her eyes and wiped the thought of the exam the next day clean from her mind. Instead she allowed the strange, haunting lyrics that slid through her brain to summon up an array of film-posterish images that put a slack, lazy smile on her face.

She had come to the realisation that there were in fact two Bellas. There was Bella before and Bella after. Fifteen years or so of before and six months of after. The after was the Bella who had discovered the soft peaceful glow of cannabis which would arrive every night like a favourite cousin to ease away the sharp edges of teenage life. To start with, smoking dope had been a once a week thing with Ellie and Tina. Sometimes in each other's bedrooms, sometimes outside somewhere, the park, the woods. Then she had asked Tina if she would get her brother to buy ten pounds worth for her and she had started to smoke on her own. She liked smoking with her friends. They always had a laugh and shared carrier bags of goodies feeling carelessly guilty with every Mars bar or Magnum. The mirror wasn't remotely happy with the new Bella. But the new Bella took care not to give the mirror much of a chance to disapprove. The new Bella didn't do crop tops. The new Bella did baggy and black and dark smudgy make up on a pale face. The new Bella was a Goth and Goths cared nothing for the skinny celebs who adorned the magazines in Tesco. Not that she saw as much of Tesco any more. Her mum was always asking if she wanted to come to help with the shopping, but Bella always said that she hadn't the time because she had loads of revision.

Both of her parents had told her how proud they were that she was putting so much time into her revision. They said that they knew how hard it was, but they pointed out that it was only a few months that would stand her in good stead for the rest of her life. They were confident that such solid revision coupled with ten years worth of excellent parent evenings would ensure first rate exam results. Her mum had tried to drop some kind hints that maybe so much study was having a detrimental effect on her daughter's figure. She no longer talked confidently of puppy fat, which would disappear when the time was right. Now she served more and more salad for the evening meal and brushed her husband's complaints firmly to one side. Bella found her mother's efforts terribly depressing. She was trying so hard and yet her carefully calorie-counted meals stood no chance of success against the stashed chocolate and crisps that were Bella's constant companion in the sanctuary of her room. The last time she had risked a proper look in the mirror without full Goth camouflage she had been appalled. She had added well over a stone in three months and there was no way that the addition could be described as puppy fat. It was fully grown dog fat and she had cried herself to sleep.

She had avoided the mirror ever since, telling herself every day that the next day would be the day that she got a grip and started the diet to end all diets. There would be exercise and sensible eating and absolutely no chocolate and crisps ever again ever. But every night she would get in from school and lay out her books for revision and sit for a few minutes feeling a sense of panic climb through her.

Then a small voice would start telling her that she was far too anxious and stressed out to be able to revise. She needed to smooth the creases out first. Just one smoke. Just a small one. Just to relax a little. Then she would be able to get on. So she would have the small smoke and she would relax. And the voice would carry on in her head, nice and soothing now. Just a quick lie down for a few minutes, then she would start work. And some music. And as the hunger would fire up, the voice would suggest a chocolate bar. In fact the voice was of the opinion that she probably needed some chocolate before starting her revision. School days were long days. Draining days. It wasn't easy to put in a full day at school and then get straight down to study. What her brain and body needed was some sugar. Some instant energy. A boost. Relax a while. Take on board some energy. Prepare the brain with some music. And then it would be tea time. And after tea the voice would suggest that one more smoke might be good idea. Just a small one. And maybe just one chocolate bar . . .

And the diet to end all diets would be put off for another day. Maybe tomorrow. Well that would be too soon. The day after. Definitely the day after. And the mirror was avoided at all costs.

Sometimes a horrible panic would be with her all day as she realised how far adrift she had become. There would be lessons that seemed almost meaningless. There would be homework that was all but beyond her. Sometimes she closed her ears to the voice and sat straight down to her revision, determined to finally make a proper start on getting ready for the exams. These were the worst of nights.

No matter how she tried, she couldn't seem to make any inroads into the mountain of work that towered over her. It was like trying to run through treacle. Where once it would have only taken her a few minutes to read and understand a page, it now took ten times longer. And when she made it to the bottom of the text she would find that she could barely remember a word that she had read. So she would read it all over again and still it was like it had been written in Japanese. It was like her brain had become a bucket full of holes and the water would run out as quickly as the tap could fill it up. Then the panic would set in and the little voice would become a very urgent big voice and she would take refuge in a smoke. A big one. And then another. And a Mars bar. And some music. And she would convince herself that the next day things would be better and she would start to get back to the way she had always been before.

But now there was no chance to start changing things tomorrow. Tomorrow was the day of her first exam. And it had taken three big joints to knock down the onrushing panic that had threatened to completely take her over. The panic was away now. It was on the floor with the three Mars bar wrappers and the empty crisp packet. It had been removed to the same place as the mirror. It was out of sight and out of mind and sleep was easing her eyes closed as the music massaged her thoughts. Lots of people managed good exams without doing any revision. She would be fine. A good night's sleep and she would be fine. And as she drifted away the little voice came up with the very sensible idea of having a smoke before getting the bus to school. It would mean she would be completely relaxed. That was important. If she allowed herself to panic, it could all go horribly wrong. But if she was relaxed, she would be fine. Everything would be fine. A breeze.

Part Three
Summer

Nightmare. Nightmare times three. Nightmare times three hundred and thirty-three, delivered with a first class stamp by a postman who played in the same darts team as her dad.

A nightmare because after spending all her school years up at the top of the class Bella hadn't passed a single exam. Not one. A very small part of her wasn't surprised. But it was only a small part. The bigger part had helped her to convince herself that it would work out OK in the end. It had to. Surely. But it hadn't.

Because as the warm morning sun had streamed through her bedroom window her dad had tapped her bedroom door and brought the nightmare to her. Maybe the day wouldn't have unfolded quite so badly if she hadn't screamed out when she had read the appalling truth of the page in front of her. The scream of course had brought both her parents up the stairs to see if everything was alright. She had locked the door and buried her head under her pillow to try and blank out the sound of their increasingly frantic enquiries. Before the clock had forced her dad to leave for work, his temper had snapped and he had hammered the door and demanded to know what the hell was going on.

But he had guessed of course. They had both guessed what had caused Bella to scream out. It had been the nightmare delivered with a first class stamp. What else? There was nothing else on that quiet sunny morning with the humming of bees outside the window. Eventually her mum decided to give her some space and Bella heard the sound of worried footsteps making their way back down the stairs to the kitchen. After a while the footsteps returned and a much softer voice announced that there was cereal and juice waiting outside the door.

By now her phone was bleeping the news that text messages were arriving. One from Tina. Two from Ellie. Bella read that they had both done OK. Ellie had done more than OK. She had surprised everyone and done really well. Soon more texts arrived asking about Bella's results and she couldn't bear to return them and after an hour or so the phone was silent.

By ten a dreadful panic had taken a grip of her. She lifted the carpet over the loose floorboard under the dressing table and pulled out dope and papers and snapped a cigarette for some tobacco. She put miles more into the joint than normal. It needed to be enough to make the nightmare go away. To make everything go away. The cold anger of her father's voice. The wretched worry of her mother's voice. The smug satisfaction of the texts. The endless miles of desolation that was her life to come. The next few years had supposed to have been all about some more school, then university, then some kind of life where there was sunlight and prospects. Now she felt like she was looking across the frozen wastes of the back end of Siberia. There would be no question of returning for the autumn term. Not after the nightmare with the first class stamp.

For a while she tried to get her head around what she would do. The college for a hairdressing course? A job on the checkout in the supermarket, counting down the minutes to a break whilst the chiselled faces of the super-thin celebrities on the magazine covers smirked at her as she weighed out the carrots and scanned the Fairy Liquid.

The first two draws gave some comfort. The morning nicotine rattled the spot and sent her dizzy. She leaned back on the wall under the bedroom window and let it ride. The fuzziness seeped through the top of her skull and for a few blessed moments the Siberian wasteland ahead of her blurred and faded. A third pull and the blurred warm place seemed for a while that it might stay with her.

But it didn't.

After draw four, the nicotine rush faded and the Siberian plain started to refocus itself. Sharper. Clearer. Bleaker. On and on and on and on to the end of her life. The nightmare was right up in front of her face in super-sharp focus and the panic came pouring back through her like a Tsunami wave. She finished the joint and rolled another with trembling fingers. But the second joint only made the focus sharper. The dull despair became razor sharp despair. And rather than standing at the edge of the great frozen plain of despair, she was now stranded right in the very middle. And all around her, in every direction, there were thousands of empty miles of ice cold nothing.

Suddenly it was overwhelming. She forced herself to her feet and put her face to the open window for some air. The act of getting to her feet had made her head spin and she screwed her eyes shut to try and stop the dizziness. Instead of stopping, it speeded up and she opened up her eyes again. Outside everything seemed so sickeningly normal. The street was weekday morning quiet. The lady from three doors up was starting a dog walk. A delivery man was ringing the door bell of the house directly opposite and looking about hopefully. A radio was playing in a back garden. The traffic out on the main road was going to and from. The every day sights and sounds of a million normal lives. People without nightmares bearing first class stamps.

And deep inside it seemed as if something was breaking. Like the snap of a great glacier. Tearing. Ripping. And finally the dam broke and the tears came. At first she managed to keep her tears silent, but after a few minutes it became impossible. Her sobs seemed to have been dragged up from somewhere deep in the earth, way down with the oilfields and fossils from times long gone. She tried to hold it back, but it was futile. She knew that the terrible sound would bring her mother and that there would be no keeping her out this time. She found the presence of mind to gather up the papers and the broken cigarettes and stuff them all into a pair of trainers in her wardrobe as the sobs turned into full on hysterics.

Panic. Terror. Panic. The door banging now. Was there still smoke in the air? She couldn't see through the tears that washed around her eyes. Would her mum smell it? She wafted a can of deodorant whilst the hammering on the door became ever more insistent. And suddenly as she turned with the spray held high she was confronted by the image she had avoided all summer. The mirror. The hated mirror. And in the mirror was a girl who looked like the fattest girl she had ever seen. And as her eyes widened and poured out tears at the sight that confronted her, the image of the faces of the magazine covers grew and sharpened. All cheekbones and sneering, mocking smiles at the girl in the joggers with the T-shirt stretched to bursting point. The girl with hair like a haystack with red staring eyes. Startled. Confused. Disgusted. Appalled. Frightened. Trapped. Her eyes. Her body. Her life. Her nightmare. And it was completely overwhelming. Impossible to handle. And in a blur she made it to the door, and unlocked it and fell into the arms of her mother. Like when she was six. Before the ice cold waters of life had frozen her to the bones.

Part Four
Autumn

The supervisor smirked as she gave the news to Bella that she was
to report to the office to see Mrs Ainsley. Mrs Ainsley was Personnel
and Bella was pretty sure that she wasn't about to be offered a pro-
motion. She had already received two verbal warnings and a written
warning had been waiting for her when she had collected her coat
the previous Friday. Same old, same old. Late. Consistently late.
And it wasn't good enough. Not if she expected to keep her position
as a checkout technician. They all assumed that she was oversleep-
ing. Well of course she was. It was the same with all the youngsters.
Pathetic. Didn't know how to get out of their pits and do a decent
day's work. No wonder the whole country was going down the pan.
No wonder everyone was shipping in Poles and Lithuanians to do all
the work. At least they knew the meaning of putting in a proper
day's graft.

Most of the other women had been occupying the checkouts since
the reign of Henry the Eighth. They hadn't much time for young ones.
Idle. That's what they all were. Idle and drugged-up to the eyeballs
most of the time. And when they weren't getting off their faces they
were busy getting pregnant so they could jump the housing queue and
get a two-bedroom flat paid for by the gullible State. Mind you, it
wasn't as if that Bella was about to get herself pregnant. Not with the
state of her. Like a beached whale. And miserable as sin. I mean look
at the face on her. Sulky cow.

They were comments that Bella would only ever half hear.
Sometimes when she walked into the canteen. Sometimes when she

was in the toilets. Sometimes when she was collecting her stuff from her locker. Conversations cut short. Hard mocking eyes. Lips curled around cheap cigarettes in disdain. She had worked in the store for two months and hadn't come close to making a friend. Nobody wanted to know her. And she knew why. It was because she was fat. Huge. Enormous. Not fit to be alive. And from the moment she started out on her first day they had all been looking at her. She felt eyes on her as the minutes dragged by as slowly as centuries. She would keep her eyes down and focus everything on scanning yet another trolley full of goods. Broccoli. Beans: cheap own brand. Sweet and sour sauce: buy one, get one free. Reduced-price mince beef. Meat balls . . . Staring. Laughing. Tittering. Mocking. Judging. Watching. And sometimes she would look up and expect disgusted eye contact only to find that they were all getting on with serving customers of their own. But they were clever. They knew how to look away the very second she looked up. But she wasn't fooled. No way. She knew full well that they were watching her. Always.

Somehow her mum had guessed she was smoking cannabis. Thankfully she hadn't actually said anything. Instead she had left a leaflet on the table in the hall by the telephone. A hint. Bella had left it for three days before she had a day off when both her parents were at work. Not that she needed to read it. She knew what dope was all about. Course she did. After all she was smoking £20 a week's worth. Nothing special about that. Everyone did. But she read it all the same and it told her what she knew already. Yeah, yeah. Yawn, yawn. Cannabis isn't addictive. Well, not physically. Psychologically maybe. Well, what was that when it was at home? Cannabis stimulates hunger. Oh really. Well fancy that. Thanks mum. I don't know where I would have been if I hadn't read this. Increased appetite can lead to increased eating can lead to weight gain . . . turn the page. Cannabis is illegal, so if you get caught a big nasty policeman will come along and lock you up and throw away the key. As if. Cannabis makes you paranoid.

Paranoid? As in maybe all the other women weren't looking at her after all. As in maybe it was all in her imagination. But what that Bev had said as Bella had made her way to the counter for a can of Coke, hadn't been in her imagination. Watch this girls. Watch her order Diet Coke. I mean talk about shutting the stable door after the horse has bolted! Sorry darling, but Diet Coke isn't going to do the trick. A JCB would be a better idea. And they had laughed. All of them. Hard laughter. Cruel laughter. And it had taken every ounce of strength she had in her to keep the tears in check until she made it into the toilets.

So paranoid? Yeah right. Like Bev really liked her after all and was getting up the courage to see if Bella fancied coming along on a girls night out to Bingo in Blackpool. What was it they said about paranoia? Just because you're paranoid doesn't mean they're not out to get you. No it wasn't cannabis paranoia. It was a bunch of vicious middle-aged cows who got their kicks from destroying her piece by piece.

She'd heard them on about how she was too fat and idle to get out of bed. Like they knew. Like they were there. They didn't see that she was up at seven because sleep was harder and harder to find in the empty hours of the night when her mind raced around in circles of depression. She could get up. It was just that she couldn't get out. She found it harder and harder to face each day. The stares. The laughter. The mocking. The mirror. The magazines. The loneliness. The broccoli. The buy one get one free sweet and sour with no artificial colouring that is an ideal way of cooking either chicken or pork . . ..

So she could get up. Getting out was the problem. Facing it all. Leaving the safety of her room for the hostility of world outside.

And each and every day she would count down the hours second by endless second until the time at last came to go home and hide away in the safety of her bedroom. Tina and Ellie had stopped ringing months earlier. Now it was just Bella. And a packet of Rizzlas and a pack of ten Mayfair and her stash. Every night she would try to smoke herself back to that first night when she had laughed until her ribs ached at the thought of Jennifer Bentley's skinny limbs disappearing down the drain. It was like something that had happened a million years ago. Another life. Another everything. The nights with Tina and Ellie when they had giggled themselves senseless and eaten boxes of Maltesers without a care in the world. She was convinced that one day she would rediscover how to smoke herself happy again.

The leaflet didn't agree. The leaflet warned that cannabis could make you sadder than sad. But she knew that the reason for her feeling so bad was Bev and her hatchet-faced cronies and a joint or two was all she had to escape the memory of their contempt. So what did the leaflet know? Whoever had written the leaflet had never done a shift on the checkouts with the broccoli and the buy one get one free sweet and sour and the eyes that were always there. The cannabis was all she had left. So the leaflet could go to hell.

Knock. Knock

"Come in."

Open door.

"Ah. Bella. Sit down please."

Sit.

"As you know Bella, we have been very concerned about your timekeeping. It really hasn't been good enough. Not good enough at all, and to be honest even when you are here on time, your commitment leaves a great deal to be desired. I'm afraid we have decided to terminate your employment. There are one or two details . . .."

Sign here. Sign there. Leave your uniform here, collect your P45 there. We're ever so sorry. We really are. We suggest that you address a few issues. We suggest you take some time to reflect. We hope that you will learn from this experience . . .

Stand up. Close door. Get coat. Avoid eyes. Never again. Outside. Bus. Walk. Home. Bedroom. Roll. Smoke. And another. And another. Because in the end what the hell did anything matter anyway? And when she had smoked every last milligram of her stash she slowly took off her shirt and skirt and stood in front of the mirror for the first time since she could remember. It wasn't Bella that stared back with vacant eyes. It was a monster. A horror. A nightmare. No wonder eyes followed her everywhere she walked. She was a freak show. A hundred years earlier she would have been signed up to be exhibited in a tent at a circus for a farthing a peep. Friends? Boyfriends? Not in a million years. Not in a trillion years. And suddenly everything was perfectly and completely clear. There was no way back. That was the message that they had all been giving her. Jennifer Bentley and the thin Mafia. The heroin-chic skeletons from the magazines. Ellie and Tina and Bev and the hard faces on the checkouts. No way back. No way forward. No way out. She was imprisoned in the body of a monster. She was locked into a life of pain.

It was time to stop.

Time to hide from the eyes that were everywhere.

Everywhere.

Everywhere.

Clock.

AUTUMN

3.37 p.m.

Thursday.

Just another Thursday.

Raining out.

And cold.

Getting dark already.

Wet pavements outside.

Wall to wall grey clouds.

Two hours 'til mum would be home.

Three hours 'til dad would be home.

Traffic splashing through puddles on the main road.

Buy one, get one free sweet and sour sauce, ideal for chicken or pork.

And mum had a new prescription of Valium in the bathroom cupboard.

The plastic tub was the magnet and Bella was the iron filings.

Door.

Landing.

No eyes now. Not here. The eyes were outside. Everywhere.

Door.

Bathroom.

Cupboard.

Deodorant. Spare razors. Toothpaste. Some nail scissors.

And Valium.

Three 10 mg per day.

A month's worth.

90.

And there really was no way back any more.

Or forward.

And the eyes were all waiting outside.

Everywhere.

Everywhere.

So Bella started to swallow the pills.

Mechanically.

Chapter Two

Stevo

Introduction

SOME THOUGHTS ON ECSTASY: A FIRST BASE AGENCY
ARTICLE FROM THE DUMFRIES STANDARD, JULY 2005

Wickerman is but one of many music festivals that have become such a fixture of the British summer. Many parents agonise long and hard about whether to allow their children to attend these events. Why? Mainly because of the terror of rampant drug use. Over the last fifteen years or so, Ecstasy has become the number one party drug of choice for the UK, so during this time of mass outdoor parties it seems like an appropriate time to consider the dangers of using it.

The basic facts. Ecstasy is a Class A drug and possessing it can get you up to seven years in prison or an unlimited fine or both. Selling it can get you life. So as you can see, the government takes it pretty seriously. On the surface of things it is hard to understand why this is the case. Is it a killer drug? Not when compared to other drugs. Ecstasy kills twenty or so Brits a year. Twenty too many, but not bad when compared to tobacco (100,000), alcohol (30,000) and heroin (3,000). So does it kill so few because not many use it? Not at all. The best guess of the government is that up to 300,000 of us pop a pill every weekend. So does it send people off the rails and violent? Again no. Most who have taken Ecstasy tell of an overwhelming urge to go about hugging everyone they meet. Not very British, but hardly a reason for locking them up for up to seven years. OK. So does it lead to crime? Again, no. It isn't addictive and people tend to use it only on the weekend or at parties. An Ecstasy pill costs between £2 and £5 which is a lot less than an hour or two in the pub – hardly a sum that will send people out in droves to rob houses and mug pensioners. (Although as I mentioned before, they MIGHT hug them).

On the surface it is pretty tough to come up with a decent story to tell our children as to why they shouldn't get out and buy a pill and get all 'loved up' rather that beating the living daylights out of each other outside a night club on the drink.

It is often said that nothing in life comes free. Sadly, it is beginning to emerge that this is very much the case with taking Ecstasy. To understand the dangers and consequences, we need to understand why it feels so damn good when people use it. Every one of us carries a store of Serotonin in our brains. When a big crisis hits us like a bereavement, the brain has evolved to release a small dose into our systems to help us deal with it. Think of it as nature's way of cheering ourselves up. This isn't just a human being thing. It's a mammal thing. We all have Serotonin – humans, dogs, rats, the whole lot of us.

Science still has a lot to learn about Serotonin, but it appears that there is a likelihood that the amount we are born with is to last us for our whole lives. Maybe this explains why some people are born happy-go-lucky whilst others are miserable as sin. The happy ones are born with Serotonin by the bucketful whilst the miserable ones have barely a drop. The first time you take an Ecstasy pill, the brain uses up the equivalent of five years of Serotonin in just a few hours which goes some way to explaining why people like it so much. But that can only ever happen once. The second, third, fourth and forty-fourth times don't come close. We only have a fixed amount of Serotonin and that first euphoric wash can never be repeated.

Now comes the scary bit. Before going any further, I should point out that scientists are still arguing about this. The way we at First Base see it, when it comes to deciding whether or not to use illegal drugs, it is always best to err on the side of caution. That means evaluating what is the worst thing that can happen. Last year a university in London produced research that suggested that the worst that can happen is a very real nightmare. In a series of interviews, they compared the state of mind of people in their mid-thirties who had been eighteen and nineteen during the big Ecstasy explosion of 1990. Their findings made for grim reading. Those who had taken Ecstasy on one or two occasions were generally four times more depressed than those who had never tried it. Those who had taken the drug on numerous occasions were up to thirty-five times more depressed. In most cases they were actually clinically depressed, signed off work and on heavy doses of medication.

So there it is. The scary part. It isn't 100% proved yet and the scientists will no doubt bicker for a few years to come. Governments are not in a hurry to spend big money on research because Ecstasy users don't commit crimes and make a public nuisance of themselves. This means that the research is being undertaken by 300,000 guinea pigs every weekend and the truth will emerge at some stage. Let's face it, people thought Thalidomide was OK until it went so very horribly wrong.

So basically we don't know. Not the scientists, not the 'know-it-all' mates who tell our kids that it's OK. I hope a few young people read this and I really hope you think twice. Because if some of the research is even half way right, then you really need to take a rain check on this one. We have had a lot of young people come in to see us, and they sit and they cry for no reason they can understand. They say that the desperate depression they feel seems to have no logic to it. And guess what. They've generally been using Ecstasy.

Stevo
Part One: 5

Big day. Huge day. The biggest day by far in the five-and-a-half-year life of Steven Taylor. It was August. It was overcast. And it was his first morning at Sunnybank Primary School. The big league. Time to move on from the day nursery with the little ones howling when they lost their teddies. Sunnybank Primary meant uniform. Sunnybank Primary meant a new bag. And more than everything else put together, Sunnybank Primary meant walking a mile to school with his big brother Dale. And his big brother's mates. Dale was starting out on his P6 year and as far as Stevo was concerned his big brother Dale was a complete God.

If the truth were to be known, Dale probably would have rather had his teeth removed with a pair of rusty pliers than make the journey to and from school with his kid brother, but both his mum and dad had made it crystal clear that it was a duty that was non-negotiable. Dad started work with a local builder at 7.30 and mum needed to be out of the house to get the quarter-to-nine bus into the town centre to start work at nine. All of which meant that it fell on Dale to ensure that Stevo was delivered on time and in one piece to the gates of Sunnybank School. Dale had let his young brother know exactly what he felt about the arrangement and it was nothing good. Stevo was given clear instructions. Shut up and try and not be noticed.

Dale had put many years of hard work into developing the right kind of credibility. He was the first on the sheet for the school team and a succession of brief flurries in the playground had been enough to consolidate his position as the cock of the P6. This position had gained him a group of followers who all met up every morning to make their way to school.

The journey was an important part of the day and a time that was rich in opportunities. The group acted as a tight knit unit and they were the bane of the younger children's lives. Most mornings at least three unfortunate victims were stopped for a bag search and any attractive items in their packed lunch boxes would be commandeered. Pockets were turned inside out to ensure that any lunch money was duly given up. Dale's group varied their route on a daily basis in order to make it as tough as possible for their targets to avoid them. By the time they arrived at school they would generally have made a solid profit from their walk – chocolate bars, cans of pop, fifty pence pieces. It was their turf and they controlled it through the age old arts of threat and intimidation. Grassing up Dale and his gang was a poor option and one which would ensure that playtime would be an utter nightmare for weeks to come. It had become an accepted fact that if you got caught and shaken down, you just had to put up and shut up and try to find another route the next day.

It was a comfortable and profitable routine that they had refined and developed for over a year and a half and having a five year old along was in no way a good addition. Dale was also conscious that having his brother along might weaken his position as top dog. So as their mum ushered them out of the door and wished Stevo good luck on his first day, Dale was focusing on dealing with any dissent that might develop among the ranks.

As it turned out he had no need to worry. His followers were all far too much in awe of him to raise any objections. More to the point, it soon became apparent that they all thought Stevo was OK. More than that, they reckoned he was actually pretty cool. Dale was so used to having his little brother as a fetcher-and-carrier that it had escaped his notice that Stevo was such a joker.

By the time they completed the journey to school, Stevo had gone a long way to establishing himself as a bone fide member of the group. He had played a full and proper part in three shake downs and had gained plenty of laughs in the process. Dale was loath to admit it, but things had gone far better than he had dared to expect. It looked as if his little bother was going to be happily accepted and his mascot status would only enhance rather than undermine his own reputation. All in all, it had been a very satisfactory start to the year. All three of their targets had been P1s making their first tentative steps into the daunting world of real school. Experience had taught the gang that this first week was always a time of rich pickings when mums would be particularly generous with lunch boxes. Nothing like an extra large Mars bar to help a terrified youngster through the first few days. It would soon wear off of course, but while it lasted there was a rich harvest to be had. Best of all was the fact that they were so utterly terrified that there was absolutely no chance of them saying a word. The morning's walk had yielded £1.50 and chocolate bars enough for the whole gang, including Stevo. Not bad. Not bad at all.

The bell was a signal for the year groups to form up in lines in the playground before being ushered into the Assembly Hall to be welcomed for a new year. It was at this point that Dale started to get a bad feeling. Once all lines were formed, a single howling figure was left alone in the middle of the playground. Sod it. It was victim number three and he was obviously taking the loss of his £1.50 and Double Decker particularly hard. Mrs Dowson scuttled over to him and guided him inside to the staff area. Not good. Not good at all. Dale exchanged a worried glance with his fellow gang members and they all entered the hall with a feeling of growing anxiety.

This feeling only grew when the headmaster, Mr Tynan, seemed to take much longer than usual to appear up on the stage. When he did finally emerge, his face was a vivid scarlet that complimented his mop of bright red hair. The man was clearly not happy. In fact he was in a towering rage and Tynan in a rage was a thing to be feared.

He took his place in front of the gathered three hundred pupils and seemed to take a small moment to gather himself. When he spoke his tone was that of a man holding himself in check. He picked his words carefully.

"I haven't had a very good start to this first day of the new school year. In fact I have had a very bad start. The worst start that I can remember in my twelve years here. I have just been talking with a very frightened young boy. He is one of our new P1 year. On his way to school he was stopped, bullied and robbed by a group of boys . . . "

Dale bowed his head and stared hard at the floor. Unbelievable. First day back and things were going down the drain before he had even walked into his first lesson. The little sod had been almost hysterical in the yard. No doubt he would have blubbed it all out. At least the boy was a stranger. Dale couldn't remember seeing him before. He must have come from a different part of the estate. He wouldn't have been able give any names but he would certainly recognise them all. He winced at the thought of what his dad would do when he was called in to be given the news. Disaster.

" . . . Worse still, the boys who did this wore the uniform of this school. In fact they are sitting in this room right now. Make no mistake, I intend to find out exactly who did this. And find out I will. And when I do . . . "

Something stopped Tynan in full flow. Dale looked up at the unexpected pause in the tirade. The headmaster's face was a mixture of anger and confusion. Dale followed the direction of his gaze until his heart felt like it missed about four beats. In the midst of the P1s the small figure of Stevo had risen to his feet. Tynan took a moment to come to terms with the fact that one of the new boys had interrupted him in full flow. No doubt the little wretch needed to pee. Christ, didn't parents teach their kids anything these days.

"What is it boy?"

"It was me sir."

"What was you boy?"

"I did it. I took the money and the Double Decker."

This really rocked Tynan. It was rare that he was lost for words but this was such a moment. In reality, his loss of words only lasted a matter of five or six seconds, but in the tensed hush of the hall it seemed much, much longer. At last he managed to speak.

"Sit down boy and don't be so ridiculous. It was a gang of older boys. Young Richmond was very specific. Who are you anyway?"

"Taylor. Steven Taylor. It was me on my own."

Tynan had been in the teaching game for long enough to know when he was being had, but the situation he found himself in was not an easy one. The boy had made the most public of confessions and there was no way that he could ignore it. Already his brain was putting the facts into line. Taylor. As in Dale Taylor. As in the little brother of the boy who was already his prime suspect. Now he could see what the game was and it was a game that he would have to play away from the fascinated gaze of the assembled school. And there was something else. The eyes. A definite glint. A glint on the first day. This Steven Taylor was clearly going to be a handful. Time to wrap it up.

"Go to my office and wait outside please Taylor . . . Now. As I was saying . . . "

What now? The wretched boy was still there. Hadn't moved a muscle. Just stood there.

"Didn't you hear me Taylor. I said go to my office and wait outside. Now!"

"Don't know where it is. It's my first day."

And a small ripple of contained sniggering whispered through the three hundred who sat on the floor of the hall. Tynan's face was going redder by the second.

"Through the door at the back and it's the door with the sign that says 'headmaster' and please don't tell me that you can't read the word 'headmaster'.."

"I don't read right well . . . "

"OUT!!!!"

And the sniggering was barely contained now.

"Quiet!!! All of you!!!"

A hush fell over the hall as every boy and girl could hardly wait to talk about what had happened. They knew as well as Tynan knew that a legend had been born and there was not a thing he could do to put the toothpaste back in the tube.

Later in the playground everyone wanted to know what 'Old carrot-top' had said once he had got Stevo in his office. And Stevo was at the centre of everyone's attention. More than that, he had won a place in the gang on ultimate merit. The fact that he was only a P1 and on his first day meant that Tynan could do nothing more than give him the darkest of dark warnings and send him packing. By the time Stevo left the office, young Timmy Richmond's cousin had explained that it would be the worst idea in the world to point out that it was Dale Taylor and his gang who had nicked his money and Double Decker. Later, when Tynan asked him once again to describe the boys who had bullied him, he had stared down at the floor and said he couldn't remember and the matter had died a death.

Three days later Tynan's face was once again redder than red when he addressed the assembly. Someone had put a carrot under the windscreen wiper of his car and when he found out who it was there would be a heavy price to pay. And again the sniggering was only just contained. And by the morning break everyone knew that it had been Stevo who had brought the vegetable to school and stuck it under carrot-top's windscreen wiper. Tynan suspected as much but couldn't prove it.

And Stevo had arrived.

Part Two
15

Stevo took a glance at his watch and found that it was the same as every other Friday. Time had ground to a halt. 3.15 p.m. He was convinced that someone must have made Maths the last period of the week as some kind of torture. The teacher was droning on about something to do with triangles and time had downed tools and stopped. Just like it did every Friday afternoon, especially when the sun was slanting down through the windows and mocking the poor sods who were chained to their desks and expected to learn all about triangles. As if it mattered. As if anyone cared. 3.16. Time minus nine minutes.

Just like always his eyes were drawn two rows forward to where Roz was sitting. Her body language spoke of attention. Where he was sprawled, she was upright. Where his focus was on the snail like progress of the minute hand of his watch, she was obviously taking on board all the stuff about triangles. And when it came to assessments she would sail through with flying colours whilst his efforts would provoke shaking heads and dark expressions.

Roseanne Brightwell had walked through the gates of Sunnybank Primary School the same day that Stevo had risen to his feet to own up to the theft of a Double Decker bar and £1.50 lunch money and sent his old headmaster's face the same colour as a tropical sunset. Within days they had become mates and mates they had stayed ever since. But things had changed over the last couple of years. No longer was Roz one of the lads. Roz was very much one of the girls, and the days when Stevo saw her as one of the lads, who was always up for a laugh, were long gone to the same place where they kept the Berlin Wall, and black and white TV, and Hollywood super heroes having a fag on the big screen. Roz was now someone who seemed to be in his mind most of the time, and it was never comfortable.

It had become the great issue of his life. In many ways it was an utterly simple issue. He wanted to ask Roz out. As in would you like to be my girlfriend out. As opposed to shall we knock about like we always have done out. As in not just mates any more. So simple, yet such a complete nightmare. Pathetic really. Ever since his epic entrance into Sunnybank Primary, Stevo had built up a reputation for his mouth. A fast talking mouth. A joking mouth. He was never a hard man like his big brother. He was a wise-cracker. Never short of a comment. He was always the one who teachers dreamed of being able to order up a visit from an Al Qaida killer cell.

But for all his mouth, the words required to ask Roz to cross the fence from being a mate to being a bird, were always out of reach. Maybe today might be the day. Let the clock crawl to 3.25. Grab bag. Leave class. A corridor conversation. A question popped. Doing anything tonight? How's about . . ? How's about what? That was the question. He had £3 to his name and that wasn't exactly going to enable him to come over all George Clooney and take her for a night in the bright lights of downtown Dumfries. It was only enough to knock about the same familiar haunts of Sunnybank Estate that they had knocked about for the last ten years. And maybe a bag of chips at the end of it. At least there would only be the two of them. Any more than two and the wardens would be there to move them on. Two's company, three's a clear and present danger. It was the new unwritten law of twenty-first century ASBO Sunnybank. Public Enemy Number One: Arab terrorists with semtex wrapped around their chests with parcel tape. Public Enemy Number Two. Teenagers. Any citizen between the ages of thirteen and twenty were viewed as an immediate threat to the quality of life of the rest of the community. They were the enemy at the gates. They were a risk at the very heart of western civilisation. They were not trusted to gather in groups of more than two and the community wardens were tasked with keeping them hidden from view.

Well if Roz said yes, they would only be two. So at least that was something. The freedom to walk the streets until the sun went down, and a bag of chips at the end of it. Hardly Romeo and Juliet, but it was all that was on the cards.

3.21.

Day dreaming of a night with Roz had given the minute hand a kick up the backside. Time had started again. The seconds were sliding down to the end of the week. Freedom from the truth about triangles. As if it mattered. As if anyone cared.

3.33.

Months and months of bracing himself for the moment and it had been a disaster. Disaster Tsunami scale. New Orleans scale. Accidental nuclear attack on Washington when all the lads on the sub were supposed to be doing was a practice drill disaster.

She had taken a moment to realise that he was actually asking her out. Then there had been mild amusement. To do what? Well, you know. Just hang out like. You know. Oh right. Not a night club then? Or a rave? She had probably meant the sarcasm to be mild, but it had felt like concentrated nitric acid. And then it had turned out that she already had plans. She was going out with Terry. You know. Used to be a mate of your Dale's. Before. Well you know. And of course he knew. Terry lived four doors down. Terry worked for his uncle who had his own building business. Terry had a Peugeot 206 with a double exhaust. And Terry was taking her to the Alpha Club with his mates. And Stevo had been stupid enough to raise the fact that under eighteen's weren't allowed into the Alpha. And she had smiled sweetly at his innocence. That's for lads darling. They never check the ID for the girls. They want as many as they can get. It's good for business darling. And lets face it, once we're all dressed up we don't look fifteen do we?

And off she went, lightly tripping down the corridor with a full and proper understanding of triangles and the prospect of a night at the Alpha with Terry bloody Mitchell and . . . He didn't want to think about the and bit. The backseat of the Peugeot 206 bit. He didn't want to think about that bit at all, so he started the process of cleaning his brain of the whole incident. Nightmare. But not a rare nightmare. It was a bone of contention that was shared by most of his mates. All the lasses were going with nineteen and twenty-year-olds who had cars and pockets full of cash and the right ID to go anywhere they pleased. And all the lads were left to kill the empty Sunnybank hours and try to dodge the wardens.

As Stevo watched her fade away down the corridor he was hit by a sense that things had suddenly moved on. Outside the sun was still pouring out of a wall-to-wall blue sky and not so very long ago they would have taken a detour to hop the wall of one of the big houses to pinch some apples out of the garden. Now she was way past nicking fruit. Now it was the Peugeot 206 and the Alpha and Dennis Mitchell. Roz was headed for the Bacardi advert whilst he was stuck in an advert warning about what would happen to people who didn't renew their tele licences. Young, free and single and the joys of Sunnybank. Great if you're a lass. Not so great if you're a lad.

The whole thing had him well on the road to getting doomed out when Sammy Teal leaned in close for a word.

"What you up to tonight?"

Stevo shrugged. "Ah you know. The usual like. Spot of water skiing then on to the casino. What else?"

"So nothing then."

"Something like that."

"Got any cash?"

"My pockets are bulging mate. Three quid. That's why I can't wait to hit the black jack tables. Why do you ask?"

Sammy tried to look completely casual as he checked up and down the corridor to make sure they couldn't be overheard. As a result he couldn't have looked any more suspicious if he had tried. He lowered his voice so that Stevo had to dip his head to catch the words.

"My brother has some eckies to sell. Five for a tenner. Mitsubishis. Proper gear like. Me, Tom, Mikey and Fed are all in for it. Two quid a head. You up for it?"

Part of him felt like a punctured balloon. All his maths lesson musing had been about something entirely different to popping ecstasy with Sammy, Tom, Mikey and Fed. It had been all about a summery Sunnybank evening with Roz played out to a filmy soundtrack. But Roz was headed down the Peugeot 206 road and his diary was a blank. He had pretty well stayed clear of drugs. He had tried a few pulls on joints and snorted up a couple of lines of speed but he was wary of the whole thing. His drugs education had been played out large and live as he had watched Dale shed the pounds and get kicked out of the house in a torrent of abuse after lifting the new DVD for a tenner bag of smack. Dale had become one of the hollow-eyed waifs who flitted in and out of the shadows on the High Street. His name wasn't mentioned in the house any more. Stevo knew that his mum still met with him under conditions of absolute secrecy to pass on £10 or £20. His dad had washed his hands completely. Stevo was under instructions to have nothing to do with his older brother, which of course he ignored. He would generally see him in the town. But all Dale ever wanted to know was how much cash Stevo had. For the last two months he had started to avoid him.

Normally the idea of a night of eckies would have been something easy to turn down. It wasn't a road he wanted to take. Fair enough, eckies were a far cry from smack, but even so. But tonight wasn't just another night. He knew that as soon as he got up to his room the sheer misery of thinking about Roz out in the 206 would start smacking him in the face like a lump hammer. Not a great prospect. In fact a lousy prospect. So maybe having a go at the eckies wasn't the worst idea in the world after all.

"Go on then. Where are you meeting up?"

"The Post Office. Eight o'clock."

"Fair enough. See you there."

For half an hour it had been the biggest damp squib he had ever known. They had got themselves all wound up. The cash had been gathered in. They had met Sammy's brother in the alley behind the library and the transaction had been completed. Then they had skirted a warden patrol and hopped the fence into the school grounds and holed up in a shadowy corner of the playground. And then with a feeling of great expectation they had knocked back a pill each.

And nothing had happened.

And so they waited a while and still nothing happened. And after quarter of an hour they had decided that Sammy's brother had stitched them and sold them a tenner's worth of dolled-up aspirins. And Stevo had slumped back against the wall and decided it just wasn't going to be his day.

Then, just at the point that he had given up on the whole thing, it started. The next few hours were a time that he never could properly explain. More than everything else, he was completely wrapped up in a feeling of almost overwhelming happiness. The other lads were all acquaintances rather than proper mates, but for the duration of that warm night they were the best mates he had ever known in his whole life. The rather faded buildings of the school became a Hollywood dreamscape. Everything was straight out of a Batman film. Fantastic. Soaring. Almost too good to get his head around. There was no particular reason why. It just was. And every single problem in the whole universe fizzled and dissolved into nothing like a sugar lump in a hot cup of tea. And why the hell wouldn't Roz want to hit the town in a 206? It was totally understandable. And he really wanted to tell her so. No hard feelings. It's OK. I don't mind. Not in the slightest. I don't mind about anything. Not now. Not ever. Not in a month of Sundays. Because everything was suddenly and completely and utterly and totally and comprehensively fine. Better than anything had ever been before.

It was all as good as it got.

And then a bit more on top. And it lasted all the way back to his bedroom and poured into his revved up brain through his headphones until sometime after four he finally drifted away to sleep.

Fair enough the next morning wasn't great. In fact there wasn't a next morning. The first he knew of Saturday was a bedside clock telling him it was past two o'clock. And he was filled with a feeling of empty bleakness that was every bit as low as the double Everest-high he had lived out just a few hours earlier. As he tried to make some sense of the familiar space around him, he started thinking about Roz and the times they had gone out nicking apples when they were seven and eight and before he knew it the camera skipped onto a picture of the new grown-up Roz all dolled-up to the nines and climbing out of a Peugeot 206 as if she was some big movie star at an opening night. And it was all so completely sad that he found that he was crying and no matter how much he tried to tell himself not to be so stupid the tears just wouldn't stop.

Thankfully his dad was out when he made his entrance into the kitchen forty minutes later and the look on his mum's face was one of ashen fear. She never said a word. All the rows with Dale had taught her not to. But her eyes said it all. Not another. Not again. Not the baby. And he tried a line about feeling as if he was coming down with something. Probably a bug. A few of the lads at school had been off. He said he was going for a lie down. And she didn't believe a word of it but still she said nothing because theirs was a house where there had been too many drug-related lies. And too many drug-related rows.

By the early evening, the great black cloud had more or less passed and life was looking up. By thc next morning the tears had become a vague memory. Nothing of consequence. What was much more relevant was recollection of magical kingdom he had visited care of £2 paid to Sammy's brother. He had never been to Disneyland but he was pretty certain that Mickey Mouse wasn't even a close second. What he was quite sure about was that he was going back to dreamland just as soon as he bought another ticket.

Part Three
25

" . . . come on for Christ's sake, wake up will you . . . "

A distant voice. A voice filtered through a couple metres worth of cotton wool. But not filtered enough. Getting through. Like dirty rainwater through a pair of shoes with holes in the soles. Irksome.

" . . . Stevo!!!"

Unavoidable. He dragged his eyes open to see Roz leaning over him looking just about as mad as he had ever seen her. Nightmare. Daylight in the window. 8.17 on the clock. A desperate wailing from the baby in the room next door. He tried to jump start his brain into any sort of action and slowly the realities of the situation started to turn up one by one.

It was 8.17.

It was Monday morning.

He needed to be in work for 9.00.

The bus had left at 8.10.

Which would mean a taxi.

And they couldn't afford a taxi because Roz had given up work to look after the little one and the mortgage still needed paying and the HP payments on all the stuff they had bought for the house were biting all the way down to the bone. So if he got a taxi he would have the mother of all rows waiting for him when he got back home. So he would have to run, but the problem was that he wasn't at all sure if he had it in him to get out of bed let alone run all the way from Sunnybank to the town centre. But he would have to because only last week a formal written warning had landed on the mat and the issue was one of timekeeping and Roz had gone completely bal-listic and asked if he realised just how hard up they were and won-dered if he realised what would happen if they got any further behind with all their payments and she just couldn't begin to under-stand how anybody could be so irresponsible with a baby just arrived . . ..

It was starting again. As be blinked away with gummy eyes it was impossible to believe that the person yelling at him was Roz. His Roz. Roz the mate. Roz the fellow apple thief. Roz who had once hit the town in a 206. Roz who in the end had agreed to become more than just a mate. And then a fiancé. And then a wife. And then a mother. And now the owner of a pair of eyes that seemed to leak pure unadul-terated loathing.

" . . . Get up . . . get up . . . get up . . .."

There were tears now. And balled fists beating a tune out on his chest. And he couldn't seem to move at all.

" . . . bloody hell Roz . . . calm down will you . . . I'm getting up OK . . . I'm fine . . . look . . . I'm moving. Give me five and I'm gone OK? Jesus . . .!"

The howling next door seemed to go up a notch or two and the sound seemed to go through his head like a rusty nail straight out of the oven. She was just crying now. Head down. Hair all over the place. Face pale and streaked.

" . . . Have you nay idea how tired I am? I mean any idea at all? Night after night and he never sleeps. And what do you do? You go out. Every weekend. And you pop your stupid pills and then you can't get up and you're late and you'll get fired and still he will never sleep. Can't you see it? Can't you see it? Can't you see anything beyond the next chemical. Jesus Stevo. What has happened to you?"

He tried to make soothing noises. He sat next to her and attempted an arm around the shoulder but she pushed him away. He dressed. He doused his face in cold water. He tried to dig out the energy to some-how run to the town centre and make it for nine o'clock.

"Look. I'll have to go love. Sorry. It's just I need to leg it, yeah?"

"Here." She held out a hand with three pound coins. "Get a cab. You'll never make it if you don't."

"Look Roz, I really am sorry. I mean..."

"Just go Stevo. Just go." A dead voice. A tired voice. A defeated voice. A voice that couldn't quite believe just how completely lousy life could be.

Nothing to say and nothing to do but go. Leave. So he left and it was only when he was a hundred yards clear of the front door that his brain was capable of registering the fact that it was tipping it down with rain and he hadn't put a coat on. He reached into his pocket and felt a surge of relief when his fingers closed on a crumpled packet of cigarettes left over from the night before. Small mercies. He heaved in a lungful of smoke and had hopes that the nicotine rush might kick start him. Instead it set off a coughing bout that escalated out of control and left him bent over with his hands on his knees trying to catch hold of a spinning head.

A taxi. He needed a taxi. Brian Skelton usually parked up by the library about this time ready to pick up a fare from the likes of Stevo who had overslept and missed the chance of a bus from Sunnybank into work. The second drag on the cigarette was marginally more successful, and he felt stable enough to start the half run, half stagger to where the taxi might be waiting.

Five minutes later he felt as if his lungs were about to disintegrate but thankfully he was greeted with the sight of Brian's venerable Carlton quietly wafting fumes into the damp air through a rusty exhaust.

"Thank Christ you're here Brian."

Brian tossed a half-read copy of the Sun onto the back seat.

"Town?"

"Yeah. Magic."

The car clunked into gear and eased into the slow moving line of traffic headed for the town.

"Big night then was it?"

"Just a bit."

"Rather you than me."

"Rather anyone than me . . . "

At which point the car became lumpy.

"Sod it. Bloody puncture."

As Brian resentfully left the warmth of the car for the cold wet of the outside world, Stevo's eyes were drawn to the digital clock on the dashboard.

8.48

Nightmare. He joined Brian outside as the cabbie was shovelling around the boot to find his jack.

"This going to take long?"

"Hell I don't know. What does it look like?"

"Look, I'm going to have to leg it…"

"Aye. Off you go. Forget the fare."

"Wow, thanks Brian, I mean we must have travelled all of a hundred yards there."

For most of his journey into work he had grave doubts that his body would actually get him there at all. But it did. For 9.21. His supervisor gave him a smug look that said it all. He had never seen eye-to-eye with the supervisor who thought Stevo was too full of himself for his own good and would do well to learn how to control his big mouth. The look said gotcha. Three warnings down, one firing to come.

There was a part of Stevo that couldn't help but welcome the idea of getting sacked. He never been particularly keen on any job he had tried. But over the last year or two it had been getting harder and harder. When he had embarked on his love affair with MDMA at the age of fifteen, the prospect of a bad morning was a price easily worth paying for the brilliance of the night before. But there had been problems more or less from the very outset of his journey.

The first problem was that no matter how many varieties he had tried or how many pills he had taken, nothing had ever come close to that first extraordinary night in the grounds of Sunnybank High School. Every weekend he yearned for a return to the fabulous dreamland he had discovered. If only for a few hours. Even a few minutes. But for ten years the dreamland had remained elusive. He still found a rush. A happiness. A burst of energy. But nothing to compare with the night of nights. The logical side of his brain insisted that he needed to come to terms with the fact that it had been a one off. A freak, once in a lifetime event. But the other part of the brain had found a Holy Grail and it was determined to pursue it with all the fervour of King Arthur and his knights.

The second problem was that although the highs were never nearly as high, the crashes sent him lower and lower. Where once it had been just a bad morning, now the trough generally lasted all the way through to Wednesday night. And the trough seemed to get deeper and deeper. For days he would have no energy at all. Worse, a black depression would fasten itself onto him and refuse to let go. He seemed to spend half of his life hiding the depression away. Roz had no sympathy for it. In fact she was sick to death of it and the first hint he gave of feeling low would be like lighting the touch paper. So day after day he would try and put on a forced act of being happy.

More and more of his life was being wasted away in a state of lethargy and black depression. Once again the logical side of his brain was fighting to be heard. The logical side of the brain had looked into ecstasy and lo-and-behold one of the main side-effects of using the pills was that the user would have to go through longer and longer crashes as time went on. And on many occasions over the last ten years the logical side of his brain had demanded that he knock the pills on the head for a while.

And he had.

Instead of the weekend jaunts with the lads to track down raves, he had spent more time with Roz. The dreaded quality time. Trips to the cinema. Meals out. Or simple nights in with a take-out and a couple of DVDs. The problem was that none of it was any good. It seemed like the only time in his life that he could ever be approaching half-way happy was once he got a handful of eckies down his neck.

The day crawled by and ended with his smug supervisor handing him a letter of dismissal which explained how the 'i's would be dotted and the 't's crossed. Outside the rain hadn't let up and by the time he completed the long trudge back to Sunnybank his spirits had sunk as low as he had ever known them. He had been in the bottom of the trough before. Many times. But it had never been as bad as this. The cold reality of his situation hammered home. He was a married man and father to a seven-month-old son. He had lost his job as a result of spending his weekends chasing a fast disappearing dream of some kind of elusive chemical heaven. He was unemployed with debt up to his ears and no obvious way of handling it. The girl who he had always loved and had become a wife, now despised him. He lived in a town where work was all but impossible to come by, especially for those with few qualifications and no references. Outside it was a world of rain and cold. Inside was a woman whose heart he was breaking piece by piece. And a son.

For an hour he chose outside. A bench overlooking an expanse of wet grass where once upon a time the wardens had stopped them playing football. Traffic splashed by and in the trees a few crows looked almost as wet and miserable as he felt. The sky moved from light grey to dark grey and the street lamps snapped on. Somewhere a few streets away a row broke out. A horn sounded. A bus passed by. The wet made its way through his clothes.

In the end there was no choice but to face it and go home and try to promise that this time it would be different.

And this time it was.

Roz wasn't interested in hearing how Brian Skelton's cab had a puncture. She wasn't interested in hearing about anything he had to say. She packed some things in cold fury and departed for her mother's house. With his son.

Leaving Stevo alone in a house with an unmanageable mortgage that felt emptier than the Gobi desert.

Part Four
35

The GP leafed through the notes in front of him and frowned. He reached out and took a sip of coffee from a cup that carried the badge of Heart of Midlothian. It wasn't his normal GP. Not that he had a normal GP anymore. An appointment was little more than pot luck. Each visit tended to mean a new face and telling the same old story. Over and over again. At last the man at the other side of the desk finished his skip reading and dropped the notes lightly.

"So. Mr Taylor. Steven, yes?"

"That's right."

"How have you been?"

How had he been? Same old question. Same old answer. Lousy. Ten years worth of lousy. Where to start with the new man? My wife walked out. The Halifax took the house. I haven't worked in ten years. She's with someone else now. A plumber. He has his own business and they have a holiday villa in Spain. Oh, and she has two more kids now. Twin daughters. Ringers for her when she was that age. I remember you see. We used to go off nicking apples together. My son is ten now. A P6. Sunnybank Primary. Same age as our Dale was when I started school. Heard about our Dale did you? Died of an overdose so he did. Eight years ago now. Just another Sunnybank junkie I suppose. Nobody shed too many tears. Let's say his funeral wasn't exactly a major social event. It rained. Well, of course it rained. It always rains. It rained that morning when Brian Skelton had a flat tyre. It was raining when Roz packed her bags and left. So how am I? How do you expect me to be? Same old, same old. Too many empty hours to fill.

Some days I just feel depressed as hell. They are the good days. Other days I spend my time thinking about suicide. How had he been?

"Not great."

"You don't feel ready for work then Steven?"

A slow bitter smile. "I struggle to clean my teeth in the morning doctor."

The frown furrowed a little deeper. "So you would like me to renew your sick line?"

Stevo nodded, his stomach knotted. No sick line would mean he would have to start going to the Job Centre every day to be sent out for compulsory interviews. As in having to face the world head on every day. And he couldn't do that. He could never do that. Not any more. There had been a time once when facing the world was no problem. Anything but. The old Stevo had embraced the world and all it had to offer. That had been the same old Stevo who had got to his feet in his first ever school assembly to take the rap for a Double Decker bar and £1.50. Now every last inch of the world carried a threat. Getting out of his flat to make it to the corner shop for some rizzlas and tobacco was a thing that took him at least an hour to prepare for. He had been gearing himself up all morning for this trip into town to see the doctor. Ready for work?

Still the frown.

"You have been on quite a lot of medication Steven. I think it might be time to started easing you down a little. These are not things you should be taking all the time. A few months at most . . .."

No.

No.

No. No. No.

Noooooooooo!!!!!

The words got tangled up in his throat and didn't want to come out right.

"I'm not sure I could manage doctor . . . I mean without my script . . . I'm not managing now . . .. I don't think . . .. Well I know . . . . Please . . .."

The notes were out again and the frown was deeper still. A pencil tapped against the desk top.

"OK Steven. I will extend your sick line for another three months, but I'm afraid it is time to ease up on the anti-depressants. I am going to cut them down for a fortnight then I'll have another look at you and we'll see how it's going."

"But doctor . . . please . . . I really can't . . . "

"Oh but you can Steven. We all can. The human being is really a very resilient beast you know. I think that you might just surprise yourself. Try some fresh air and exercise. Long walks. Plenty of fruit. Vegetables. It all works you know. Chemicals are not the only answer Steven."

The man was on his feet now. A smile on his lips and his eyes on the clock. Hand extended.

"See you in a couple of weeks. Remember what I said. Long walks Steven. Fresh fruit."

Only when he was outside the surgery and on the pavement did Stevo realise that he had been halved. Halved! That was the man's idea of cutting down a bit. He collected the script from the chemist with a biting sense of desolation. Already he had been feeling about as bad as it seemed possible and now he had been halved. It didn't bear thinking about.

The clock outside told him it was already past two and he was due to collect Thomas from the gates of Sunnybank Primary at three. It was their fortnightly time together. Once upon a time it had been more, but he had missed too many appointments. He tried to explain to Roz that there were days when he just couldn't face leaving the flat. She had no idea what it was like. The fear. The black misery. But Roz was never in the mood to hear any of it and in the background the plumber would hover and his face made it clear that he would love to flush Stevo down a giant toilet. As Thomas got older, the visits got harder. What to do? He had hardly any money and no transport. It was generally a walk about and a 'happy meal' at McDonalds whilst both of them willed the time away.

He was on a last warning now. Any more missed appointments and that would be it. Roz was adamant. Enough was enough. What he needed to do was to sort himself out and stop feeling sorry for himself all the time. Once he had given her an article that he had cut out from one of the Sunday papers which explained how new research suggested that regular ecstasy use caused a depletion of serotonin levels in the brain which meant there were thousands out there in the same boat as he was. But she had screwed the paper up and binned it and told him that she wasn't interested. She had stopped being interested many years earlier. There would be no more excuses. He either turned up on time or that was it.

Turning up on time meant a walk to the school and an hour was more than enough. A bus was out of the question for it would mean there wouldn't be enough cash left for a 'happy meal'. That was a joke. A meal to make you happy. A pill to make you happy. The happy pill. The pill that had once turned the deserted grounds of a school into a wonderland. A pill that had always promised that one day it would take him back there. Like some half-remembered holiday from childhood when the world had seemed to be forever sunny. Instead the pill had taken him all the way down to a desolation that knew no end.

An hour to walk. Two hours of strained contact. He hated the word contact. Cold. Brutal. A Social Services word. A father meets up with his only son once a fortnight and they called it contact. And because they only met up once a fortnight, they never had anything to talk about any more which meant that the minutes they spent with each other dragged by as slowly as a maths lesson at the end of the school week. He knew that Thomas really didn't want to see him much any more. It was there in his eyes as he picked his way through his chips. And when the contact was over Stevo would feel worse than ever. Some father. Happy meal, sad dad. Pathetic dad. Loser dad.

He arrived at the school gates at five to three to find Roz was waiting for him. There was something in her eyes. Something very sad. She didn't really want to speak to him. To say it. Whatever it was. Her eyes were fixed to the pavement when she spoke.

"I'm afraid Thomas doesn't want to see you Stevo. I have tried to talk him round. Honestly. I really have. It has been coming for months. He's ten now. Not a baby any more. I'm sorry Stevo. Really. I did try."

He joined her in staring down at the paving stones.

"I know you did Roz. Thanks. If I was him I wouldn't want to see me either. Who would?"

The tears were coming on fast. Time to go. Time to hide. Time to lock the world outside. He was turning when he felt her hand on his shoulder. He tried to keep his head down, but she saw the tears splashing from his eyes.

"Oh Stevo, what happened to you?"

And she wrapped herself round him and tried to squeeze out the cancer that had eaten everything away. But he was like a worn out sponge and after a while she released him and he saw that she was crying as well. Time to go. Time to hide. Time to lock the world outside.

"Bye Roz."

He turned and as he walked he could feel her eyes on him. When he closed and locked the door of his flat, he stood for a while and took in his last sanctuary. Dirty plates. Piles of unwashed clothes. Nothing much in the cupboards. He had left the TV on when he had left the house and now some American game show was filling the silence that seemed to leak up from under the floorboards.

Long walks and fresh fruit. A prescription halved. A life to lead.

For what?

"Oh Stevo, what happened to you?"

Wonderland happened. That's what. Wonderland for a few incredible magical hours and then his visa had been withdrawn. There was no more wonderland. Not any more. There was just a cold empty filthy flat and a prescription halved and some guy from the somewhere in nowhereville Wisconsin showing off $3000 worth of dental work and asking if a housewife from Colorado had any idea what the capital of Sweden was.

It was Stockholm.

And this was his life and it was suddenly very clear that it wasn't worth living any more. He had three bottles of Paracetamol in the kitchen cupboard. He had a halved prescription in his pocket. He had a half bottle of Vodka on top of the tele. It was time to go. Maybe not to wonderland.

But anywhere was better than here.

Chapter Three

Chelle

Introduction

GOOD GUYS AND BAD GUYS AND TRYING TO
TELL THEM APART: A FIRST BASE AGENCY ARTICLE
FROM 'DUMFRIES BY NIGHT', SEPTEMBER 2005

Think onion. And think layers. Down and down you go with your eyes filling up with tears as each layer comes off to reveal the one underneath. It is the same with the heroin story, only the tears are a different kind.

Layer one. User. This is generally someone who has had something or other really bad happen in their life and a helpful mate has suggested some medication that keeps all the nightmares away. And it costs a tenner a go. Smack. 'H'. Kit. Brown. Whatever. About one-fifth Diamorphine and four-fifths of whatever is kicking around in the dealer's kitchen that looks about right. Good guy or bad guy?

Layer two. The street dealer. This is usually the guy at layer one plus three or four years. By this time the medication is costing £40 a day and shoplifting is a big no-no. So how to make the £40 a day with no job? You deal to a few mates and cover your own habit out of the profits. Good guy or bad guy?

Layer Three. The guy who brings the stuff into town. In the eyes of the public this guy usually seems pretty stand up. Maybe he'll play golf. Maybe he'll have a shop or something. There will be a nice car and nice house and nice kids going to a nice school. And nice holidays and nice donations to nice charities given with a nice smile. (No. He won't have to wait for a NHS dentist) As a rule these guys wouldn't touch a bag of smack in a million years. They are businessmen on the greatest gravy train since the Klondike gold rush. Good guy or bad guy?

Layer four. The nation-wide wholesaler. A couple of hundred years ago the British Empire sent raw materials from all over the world to the UK to be made into finished products in new-fangled buildings called factories. It was called the Industrial Revolution and one city more than any other built up expertise in importing and distributing. It's the one with Pier Head and the Liver Building and the newly crowned Champions of Europe. Liverpudlian importers learned their trade on sugar and slaves, then they moved on to cotton and bananas. Now they distribute most of the UK's heroin. Good guys or bad guys?

Layer Five. The shipper. As often as not this guy will be Turkish. Like his Liverpudlian colleague, he will be drawing on a long, long tradition. In his case the tradition goes back not hundreds of years, but thousands. The produce of the East was flowing through Turkish merchants when Alexander the Great was in his prime. Spices, silks, heroin. It's all the same. Commodities that we in the west want and those in the east produce.

Layer six. The feudal baron. This guy will be an Afghan. Almost all of the heroin that hits our streets starts in an Afghani poppy field. To get a handle on this guy, you need to think Robin Hood films and think Sheriff of Nottingham. He will have a bunch of lads around him all armed to the teeth and he will rule the roost over a couple of hundred square miles of countryside. Any poppy farmer who doesn't sell their crop to him gets a bullet in the back of the neck. It is called a closed market. These chaps had a torrid time of it in the nineties. That was because the Taliban took control of things in Afghanistan and they believed that growing poppies for heroin was against the Koran. So they started putting bullets through the back of the Feudal Barons' heads. But in 2001 it all came good again. Some crazy guys drove some planes into American buildings and the good and the great decided that the Taliban had to go. So the feudal barons were all signed up by the CIA to join the great crusade and their part of the bargain was that they got their old business back. The Taliban were duly kicked out and this year's poppy crop will break all records. One of these gallant friends of America, Tony Blair and the free world, now has 4,000 tonnes of pure heroin in his warehouse. It is enough to keep Great Britain going for the next forty-five years. It has a street value of two hundred billion pounds. Good guy or bad guy?

Layer seven. Grower. This guy will have a wife and a few kids and a pretty dour sort of a house. If he grows anything other than poppies he will get shot through the back of the head. So he grows poppies and if he is lucky he'll make enough for the family to eat. He works fifteen hours a day and he will probably have never watched a television in his life. Good guy or bad guy?

Answers. Who the hell knows? Maybe you're a bad guy unless you might be of use in the War on Terror?

Chelle

Sometimes she had read in magazines about how important it is to try to take time out for reflection. Or maybe she had seen it on the tele. Life guru stuff. How to deal with the modern world stuff. Take a step back to breathe in some clean pure air and claim a bit of brain time. Take stock of your life. Assess your well being. Turn off the TV. Put the chores to one side. Eat fresh fruit. Find some space of your own.

Well she had her reflection time now. Lots and lots of it. The cell in the Loreburne Street Police station didn't have a clock, and the watch her Gran had given her had been sold on years ago. How many years? It seemed like thousands, somewhere back in the time before the Roman Legions had reached Carlisle and decided to build a wall rather than go any further. Her sixteenth birthday had pretty well been the last day of her old life. Her first life. The life where she had been Michelle Williams. Before she had become Chelle. Before she had started out on the dark road.

But when she thought about it, it really hadn't been all that long after all. Only four-and-a-half years. It just seemed longer. The sixteen years of Michelle had passed in a blur. The four-and-a-half years of Chelle had been like a lifetime. Maybe the miles counted treble on the dark road. Now there was a reflective thought. A lifestyle magazine editor would no doubt have approved of such reflection.

Chelle didn't generally do reflection. Reflection equalled pain. Always. Reflection meant having to come to terms with how horribly wrong everything had gone. It meant tears of regret and sleep that would never come to take the pain away. So reflection was a thing that she would always kill like an irksome fly. Reflection and memories. Guilt and regret. Fear and loathing. She would kill the whole lot in one go with a firm press of the needle. And then there would be peace.

But now the memories were going to come whether she liked it or not. Because they didn't do needles in the holding cells of Loreburne Street police station. They did two 60 mg dihydrocodeine tablets every six hours or so. If you were lucky. Just about enough to stop the stark walls of the cell being covered in vomit. The first time she had endured a night in custody, the tablets had more or less kept the pain at bay. When had that been? A handful of DVDs lifted from Woolworth's. A year ago? No. Longer than that. Must have been two years ago. Then she had been locked up at four in the afternoon and there had been only one night of the horrors to endure before being delivered to the Sheriff at ten o'clock the next morning. But then she had not been using much more than a bag of heroin a day. Two when the Giro landed on the mat. Three if a birthday card emerged from the lost world of Michelle. At the time, she had thought that two tablets were nothing. She hadn't slept a wink and had been overtaken by a frantic claustrophobia that lasted the whole night through. But in hindsight she realised that there hadn't been a great deal of pain.

Not like this time.

This time the police car had pulled up next to her at six o'clock on a Friday night. A warrant served. The sickening thing was that the warrant was for nothing. A breach of community service. They could have served it any time they pleased, but they had chosen six o'clock on a Friday night. Well of course they had. Because that meant she would have to sweat it out all the way through to ten o'clock Monday morning. Sixty-four hours. Three thousand eight hundred and forty minutes. Two hundred and thirty thousand and four hundred seconds. Eternity times a thousand plus the history of the universe.

How long had it been now? Her breakfast tray was still sitting waiting for her. How long had it waited? Three hours? Maybe less. It had to be mid-morning. About ten. Eleven. Which meant that it would be two whole days more before she would be taken to stand in front of the Sheriff. The thought made her eyes prickle with tears. It was such an impossible amount of time. And she knew that no matter how bad she felt now, it was nothing compared to what was to come. She had banged up her last bag at four o clock the previous afternoon. There would still be plenty of heroin in her system, but it would get less with every hour that passed. Which meant that the pain would get worse with every hour that passed. And she had been at it for long enough to know that day three was the worst. The most unbearable. And it all lay ahead of her.

It was a toss up as to which pain was worse. The physical pain was building steadily now. It was all over her. A biting, aching, cramping misery that seemed to climb into every pore of her body. It was in her bones and eyes and arms and legs. Complete. Utter. And yet it wasn't impossible to handle. Nearly so, but not quite. Someone had once told her that women handled withdrawal better than men. Women were born with a much greater ability to handle pain because they were designed to deal with childbirth. Maybe it was true. Maybe it wasn't. It didn't seem so. It didn't seem possible that she could feel worse. But somehow it was just about controllable.

Not so the mental pain.

The memories that were now starting to pour down on her. Memories that swarmed like some great native army armed to the teeth and desperate for the taste of blood. It had been years since she had actually enjoyed the feeling that heroin gave her. Now all she craved was the escape from all the nightmares. Once upon a time she had actually considered using kit to be a recreation. Unbelievable. Once upon a time it had seemed like a choice rather than a need. That stage hadn't lasted long.

Trying to fight off the memories was becoming hopeless. The bare cell offered no distractions. Already she had counted the bricks and read every bit of graffiti left by others who had killed the empty rattling hours. Now as the heroin retreated, her brain was left as exposed as a Ukrainian city waiting on an advancing Nazi army. She wanted to be one of the ones who bundled up all her belongings onto a hand cart and set out after the retreating Red Army as it fled into the East. But it wasn't an option because a great big metal door with a peephole stood between her and any hope of retreat. She was one of the ones who were left in the overcrowded hospital with wounds that made it impossible for them to be evacuated. Trapped. Locked down. Exposed. Wide open. And slowly but surely the memories were nudging closer and closer, like snub-nosed Panzer tanks with the gunners staring down from the turrets with the leering grins of serial killers.

She lay back on the hard bed and stared up into the harsh ceiling light. What was the point in fighting? The memories had arrived now.

They were in the cell with her. All around her. Memories with hard cruel faces. Memories in black caps bearing the skull and crossbones of the SS Einsatzgruppen death squads. Patient. Ready now to start the torture and the torture would last all the way to Monday lunchtime and the chance of a relieving bag.

The first memory took her back to age sixteen. When it had all changed. When it had all gone wrong. Before then her life had been straightforward. Sheltered. The family had moved to Dumfries and Galloway from Fife when she had been three years old. Her dad worked for the Forestry Commission and one of the great joys of her life were the times when he would take her with him for the day. They would drive for miles in his Land Rover through millions of pine trees. They took the rough tracks where those without a 4x4 would never dare to drive. They left the world behind and entered Hansel and Gretel land with cheese sandwiches wrapped in tin foil and Club biscuits and a flask of coffee for him and Coke for her. Her life had been dominated by the countryside. With her father it was the forest. With her mum it was their two horses which lived in the paddock that had come with the house. Her Primary School had been home to thirty-three pupils and surrounded by fields filled with milk cows. For years the horses had been at the very centre of her life. Feeding and grooming and riding. These had been times she had shared with Jenny who lived on a small farm three miles up the road that ran by their house.

Then, when she turned twelve, the world started to open up a little. Every morning a taxi would take her and Jenny to the High School ten miles away in the town. And suddenly there were more pupils in the classroom than there had been in the whole of her primary school. There were some new friends, but none like Jenny. Sometimes there would be parties and birthday outings, but not often. Every night the taxi would take her back home to her horses. For most of her time at High School it had seemed as if she was barely noticed.

Compared to all the girls from the town, she was quiet. Reserved. A gawky girl who was all arms and legs with straight mousy hair and a brace in her mouth until she was fourteen. When the other girls did notice her, it was usually to make fun of her flat chest. She didn't particularly like school, but she didn't hate it either. It was just school. She was a better than average student and it was always assumed at the family dinner table that college awaited a few years down the line.

CHELLE

As the last rearguard of the heroin melted away, the memories started to firm up and gain a clarity.

Sixteen. The turning point. It would have been easy to blame it all on that first night at the Town Hall disco, but in truth things had been changing for a while. It was when she was sixteen that she stopped being gawky and started being slim and the boys in the class had started to take an interest. There were invitations that she had never taken up, but they had awakened her interest. Jenny had been to the Town Hall disco four times before she finally persuaded Michelle to give it a go.

At the time it had seemed like the most magical place she had ever been. Lights and what seemed like hundreds of people of her own age and dancing and the base of the music rattling her skull.

And Tony Hopkins.

Tony had always been one of the main players in the classroom. He was self-assured and never short of words. In the playground he was in with the crowd. On the football field he was on the right side of midfield. And when Michelle was ever on the edge of a chatting crowd of the girls, he was as often as not at the centre of the conversation. What Tony Hopkins did was worthy of discussion. Especially when it came to who he was going out with. Before the Town Hall disco she had never exchanged a single word with Tony Hopkins despite sharing the same classroom for four years.

But on that night of nights he had made a beeline for her, drawn by the sight of how she suddenly looked in her jeans and T-shirt and the make up that Jenny had applied in the toilets. No longer the gawky girl with the brace. Almost no longer Michelle. Hindsight told her this was the moment that she reached the gates of the world of Chelle. Nothing all that dramatic had happened that night. Well, not when viewed from a distance of four-and-a-half years. But at the time it had seemed more dramatic than a full on nuclear strike as Tony had found a secluded corner and snogged her half to death.

A week later Tony had introduced her to some mates of his and he had called her Chelle. Maybe that was the real turning point. The very first time she had been addressed by the name that came to represent part two of her life. Tony's brother Pete had a car and it became like a chariot to a whole new world. They went all over the place at weekends. As far as her mum and dad were concerned, she was always at the disco in the Town Hall, whereas in truth they were screaming around the countryside to other small towns where Pete would park up next to other small cars with blue lights shining down on to the tarmac and booming fat exhaust pipes. And one by one she started doing the things she had always promised herself she would never even think about. First up it was fast-swigged bottles of WKD and Bacardi Breezer. Then she started saying yes to offered cigarettes. Then it was yes to passed joints. Then ecstasy pills and sharp lines of speed that all but popped her eyes out. And none of it mattered in the slightest because she was Tony Hopkins girl and they owned the quiet roads of the night.

It had taken a month or two for the rows at home to start, but once they started they were soon something that happened every day. Why was she neglecting the horses? Why didn't she ever see Jenny any more? How could it be that she suddenly had so little homework when it was only a few weeks until her exams? Michelle would have withered under the questions of her parents. Not so Chelle. Because Chelle had face. Chelle rode the night roads to towns where more and more knew her name. Chelle was Tony Hopkins girl and she didn't do being cowed. No chance. She was an up for it girl. She was an in-your-face girl.

And the exams had come and she had been blown clean out of the water. Her parents had gone along to the school to see if she could return for another year to have another go. And that was when the curtain was drawn back a little. Michelle's parents wanted to know about Michelle, but for several months the teachers had become familiar with Chelle. And they didn't want Chelle back. No thank you. Chelle was disruptive. Disrespectful. A bloody nuisance. It wouldn't be fair on the younger ones to have her back. It was all a great shame of course. They suggested that Michelle's parents should talk to their daughter about Tony Hopkins. They suggested that the local college would be a more appropriate place. But not the school. No thank you very much.

Her parents had indeed talked to her about Tony Hopkins who in truth had been a worry to them for several months. And Chelle had blown a gasket and told them to mind their own business and she had thrown clothes into a bag and stormed out of the house. Later she had learned that her mum had wanted to chase her and drag her back, but her dad had said it would be better to let her have her head. Let her see how it was in the big wide world. She would be back soon enough. Maybe a splash of cold water in the face might be for the best. After all, where would she stay?

What her dad didn't know was that Tony's brother Pete had hooked up with Tina who was nineteen and already had two kids and had been allocated a three bedroom flat on Sunnybank Estate in Dumfries. Tony had moved in as soon as he had finished school and Chelle had been there almost every weekend. So somewhere to stay wasn't a problem. Somewhere to stay was easy. Her mum and dad had thought she would be back within a day or two.

Wrong.

Her mum and dad had believed that the whole Chelle thing was just a passing phase and that Michelle would soon return and everything would be like it had been before.

Wrong.

Michelle was gone.

The time of Michelle was over. The era of Chelle had begun.

And for two months of what seemed like endless sunshine it had all been a dream. Freedom was absolute. They hardly ever went to sleep before the light of the dawn filled the flat and more often than not they didn't get up until late into the afternoon. Life became hazy and it pretty well escaped her notice that pills and powders came to dominate just about every waking hour of the day. In order to keep the all summer long party rocking along, she drained the savings account she had opened with money left by her Grandmother who had died when Michelle was twelve. It quite escaped her notice that she was the only one who was contributing to keeping the good times rolling, and when the account finally ran dry during the last week of August, the party was very much over.

Now she finally started to become accustomed to the cold water of real life that her dad had been convinced would bring her home after a day. Things had started to change fast. Pete's beloved car which had carried them all down the quiet country lanes of the night was sold and they were night riders no longer. It was increasingly apparent that Pete and Tina had problems. Three bags each a day of heroin problems. Chelle learned never leave her purse about the place. One by one her possessions went missing. Jewellery. A CD player. A bank card. Each time the house was filled with screaming accusations and even louder screaming denials. And every time it was laid squarely on the line. If Chelle didn't like it, then Chelle could get lost. Find your own place then. If not, then the best thing she could do was to keep her big mouth shut.

Night after night she nagged at Tony to help her to find a place of their own, but he wasn't interested. He pointed out the birds and the bees. They were sixteen. They were the least important of statistics. Sure, if she had a kid it would be different, but she didn't have a kid. Which meant they were at the bottom of the housing list. No points. So it was best that she kept her big mouth shut.

It was the first time that she started to know what it was to be trapped. She had nowhere to go except Tina's, and Tina would rob her every chance she got. Or at least that was what she had believed until one day she came out of the bathroom to find Tony frantically delving through her bag.

She had been half way through saying something along the lines of how dare you when he had spun round and laid her out with a right hander. Then he told her how it was. Shouted it from three inches with spit landing in her shocked face. It wasn't just Pete and Tina who were on the smack. It was Tony as well. Hadn't she noticed? Course she hadn't because she was a stupid little bitch from the back end of nowhere. And it was about time she woke up and smelt the coffee. This wasn't some kind of poxy Disneyland. This was the here and now and if she didn't like it she could just pack her bag and get lost.

She had stayed in the room all afternoon, huddled and tearful. He had left with her last £10 note and it was almost midnight before he returned. She spent those hours wondering whether he had in fact given her advice that she should take. Maybe it was time to pack her bag and return to the small house with the paddock that was home to two horses and three miles down the road from where Jenny lived. But going home would mean telling her mum and dad that she had spent every penny of the money that Gran had left her and owing up to the fact that every piece of jewellery that had been left in the same will had been stolen and sold on. And the thought of it was just completely unbearable, and so it was that later on she crept out of the room and joined the others in the filthy lounge.

And when Tony made a peace offering that was burnt on foil she accepted it and joined their world.

Over the next months she was no longer an outsider. They never stole off her because she had nothing for them to steal. Her life developed a routine. A structure. No longer did she lounge about in bed until the late afternoon. Now she was up early and taking care in front of the mirror. Her appearance was suddenly very important. It seemed ironic that Chelle now spent her days looking like Michelle had once looked. She wore conservative clothes lifted from the rails of Marks and Spencer. She was the epitome of the young girl from the country in the town for a day's shopping. It was the look that kept the eyes of the security men on the doors of the shops looking the other way. They were ever vigilant for the skin-and-bone junkies with clothes which hadn't been washed in a while. In fact that was exactly the way that Tony looked when he walked up and down the rails in the shops making sure that he was the centre of attention whilst Chelle stuffed as much as she could into her bag.

For a few months things had been bearable. There were times when she refused to go out and steal for them. These were the worst of times when her three housemates would turn on her and the abuse would usually end in a beating from Tony. He would always take care to leave her face untouched. A bruised up face wasn't good for business. So it was that the butter wouldn't melt in the mouth act kept four habits going for several months, but all good things have to come to an end. The end was the handful of DVDs in Woolworth's and Chelle ended up in the holding cells of Loreburne Street police station for the first time and the following day the Sheriff fined her and said that next time he wouldn't be anything like as lenient. The next time he upped the ante and gave her a hundred hours of community service. As a country girl, she hadn't found planting trees and collecting litter any great hardship. The real problem was that her photo had now been passed around the shops and the butter wouldn't melt in the mouth act had passed its sell by date.

Things started to slide as all four found keeping up with their collective habit harder and harder. Tina and Chelle had done all they could. Tina had played the two kids card for all it was worth and chased in every penny that the caring State had to offer. Now the State wasn't so caring any more. The State smelt a rat and social workers and health visitors became regulars at the door. The gravy train had pulled out of town. Day after day they forced her out to try to shop lift, but her face was far too well known. So it was time for the men of the house to do their bit.

This meant the brothers starting out on a new career with Double D. Double D was the currant Mr Big of the Sunnybank drug scene. His early life as a bus driver gave no clues that he would one day make it all the way to the top of the local tree. If anyone had looked closely at Donald Dennison in the days when he ferried passengers to and from Dumfries from the surrounding towns and villages, they would had seen little to suggest the career which would bring him so much success. The clues would have been found in brief, vicious fights on Friday and Saturday nights when he was full of several pints of Tennant's chased down by an equal number of whiskies. By the time he was in his mid-thirties, it was an open secret that it was not a remotely good idea to pick a fight with Donald Dennison. It wasn't that he particularly looked the part. Years of lager had settled on his waist and he was Mark and Sparks casual as opposed to Armani. But when it came to a fight, he always had more up his sleeve than any of his opponents anticipated. First up, he was as quick as a snake. Second, and easily most important, he had absolutely no qualms at hurting people. In fact it was something that gave him great pleasure.

It was a fairly rare thing that he started a fight. What was completely usual was that he finished it, and almost inevitably an ambulance was required to take away the debris. It all finally went wrong in 1998 when he hospitalised a visiting football fan in front of a CCTV camera and was sent away for a year-and-a-half. That meant that at the age of thirty-seven a change of career was inevitable. The bus company made it clear that they had no interest of giving him his job back when his time was done. His wife took the opportunity to hop town and eventually hitch up with a colour sergeant from a regiment barracked in Shropshire.

Like many others before him, Double D found that prison opened his eyes to hitherto unknown opportunities. After three trademark fights in the exercise yard, his reputation was assured and other cons wanted to know him. Night after night he quietly learned the ins and outs of the most lucrative trade on planet earth, and once he was released he used his contacts to set up in business as a purveyor of Class A narcotics to the buoyant customer base of Sunnybank Estate.

It only took him two years to become the undisputed top dog and by the time Pete and Tony Hopkins approached him for work, his position was unassailable. Double D had several things going for him which ensured that he was able to stay well ahead of the competition. Firstly and mostly obviously, he was violent to the point of being psychotic and nobody in their right mind was about to cross him. Second, he had a sly intelligence that had never been remotely stretched during his time as a bus driver. Now it was given full rein and he applied all the lessons and advice he had picked up care of Her Majesty to ensure he stayed comfortably clear of the clutches of the police. Thirdly and most importantly, he never touched the goods himself. The products he sold held no attraction whatsoever to Double D. Every day he saw the results of the chemicals he sold and how they reduced people to the state of virtual beggars. No way was he about to embark on that particular road. He was more than happy to hold court in the local pub with his pints of Tennant's and whisky chasers. Just like he always had.

The Hopkins brothers met his employment requirements well enough. At twenty and eighteen respectively they were the right kind of age. A combined habit of eight, tenner bags a day was enough to make them willing to do anything but the heroin had not yet reduced them to the kind of walking corpses that attracted too much attention. And they were both bright enough to handle their accounts reasonably well.

So it was that Pete and Tony became local dealers with a franchise from Double D that enabled them to feed their habits with ease as well as keep Chelle and Tina going. Suddenly Chelle found herself a long way down at the bottom of the pecking order. Pete and Tony were fully occupied selling the gear. Tina still had cards to play. After all, their base was her flat and she never let the lads forget it. She was in charge of the cutting and bagging side of the operation which meant that she had plenty of opportunity to dip into the goods herself. Chelle was left to mind Tina's kids, and whilst the others were able to escalate their habits to ten bags a day and more, Chelle had to make do with the leftovers. Whenever she begged not to be locked up in the flat with the kids she would get a beating. Whenever she pleaded to be given a fairer share of the cake she would get a beating.

This was when the in-your-face Chelle started to wither and die. Day after day she was left alone with the children. Hours of mindless daytime TV accompanied a crawling clock as she waited for the other three to return. Sometimes they would not come back until after midnight. Sometimes they wouldn't come back at all and she would spend the night balled up on the settee fighting the growing panic of withdrawal. A pitch-black depression unlike anything she had ever known settled into the marrow of her bones. She was trapped. Locked in. No money. No friends. No hope. She was like a beaten dog chained into a kennel. The door was always locked but she knew she could make it out of the window. But then what? Where would she go for a bag? And no matter how bad things got she could never find the heart to leave the two children. For the first time her mind started to turn to the idea of suicide. A release from the nightmare. No more beatings. No more nights of grinding pain. No more loneliness. No more tears to shed at the memory of her mum and dad and Jenny and the two horses in the paddock. On two occasions she ran a bath and had a knife ready but on both occasions she wasn't quite ready to cut the cord. When the time came, the flickering hope of the next bag was enough to pull her up at the edge of the cliff and slowly step back.

Then one night they didn't come back at all. Nor for the whole of the next day. Nor the next evening. When the door was eventually knocked in it was by a social worker accompanied by two policemen. She was resigned to the fact that the game was up. Resigned to a return to the cell in Loreburne Street. But they hadn't come for Chelle. They had come for Tina's children. One of the policemen explained that Tony and Pete and Tina had been caught in possession of an amount of heroin that was a country mile more than what could be passed off as for personal use. They were on remand and there would be no bail. They were going down. All the way down.

When they left her weak and shaking, the front door was hanging drunkenly on its hinges. She was a prisoner no more. And the only way to the next bag was to get out and get it herself. For a few days things were a little better. The Chelle who re-emerged from her prison bore little resemblance to the Chelle whose picture was still in the hands of the security men on the doors. The gawky girl had become the slim girl. And now the slim girl had become the semi-skeleton. Instead of designer clothes from boutiques she now stole frozen joints of meat from cheap food stores. Somehow she managed to dredge up enough cash to keep the demons at bay.

Then, three nights after the children had been taken, the door was once again pushed in. This time it was a messenger sent from Double D and the message was clear. Tony and Pete and Tina had been caught with £3,000 of Double D's smack and that meant that there was a debt. Now that the others were away for a while, the debt was on her and Double D wasn't a person who waved debts. Chelle was given a simple choice. She could work to clear the debt. Or she could have her face cut.

Chelle opted to work to clear the debt.

Once again the work required her to dress up in her country girl on a day out guise. Her job involved a bus to Carlisle and a train to Liverpool where she would collect packets of heroin to be hidden deep inside her body. Then there would be a train back to Carlisle and a bus back to Dumfries. Double D kept a flat on the far side of Dumfries from Sunnybank. She was given a key and told how the floorboard in the back bedroom was loose. She was to leave the hero-in under the floorboard and return home. Someone else would check that all was in order and much later an envelope of heroin would be posted through the letterbox by way of payment. For the very first time Chelle had enough heroin to keep the nightmares at bay.

But that was all it did. All the beatings and the times locked away in the flat had left her damaged. Every shred of confidence had been stripped away. The whole world had become a place of threat and fear. She never went out unless she had to. She ate less and less and the flesh melted away leaving tired white skin stretched tight over her bones. When the order came to take a trip to Liverpool it would take all of her strength to summon up the nerve to leave the house and make the journey. Only the constant terror of a knife being taken to her face was enough to galvanise her into action. For months on end she barely spoke to a soul. She hid away. Paralysed. Hibernating.

In the end it lasted well over a year. It had seemed as if it would last forever. Double D was an untouchable. He was perched high up in the branches, way beyond the reach of the long arm of the frustrated law. Double D was never in the same room as any of his merchandise. He was seldom within a mile of where the stashing and cutting and bagging was going down. He placed all his orders through his mobile phone and he went through at least five SIM cards a fortnight. His business thrived through the efforts of an endless stream of Tonys and Petes. Desperate ones. Disposable ones. Of use for a few months, and then off the pay roll as they disappeared through the prison gates. So long as Double D thrived, Chelle would be required to make the journey south to collect his goods. She had no idea whether the debt left by Pete and Tony was clear. After a while it was fairly clear that it would never be clear. She was chained to the treadmill by the need for the envelopes pushed through her letterbox. The envelopes that kept her safe. The envelopes that kept the demons at bay.

Then one day she passed the end of the close where Double D lived to find it filled with flashing blue lights and she knew that things had come to an end. She had turned and walked away and tried to get her head around the consequences. No Double D meant no more envelopes. But then she realised that she had a bolt-hole. The flat on the far side of town. It would be her sanctuary. And, best of all, there was a whole consignment of Scouse heroin hidden under the bedroom floorboard. Plenty to keep her going for as long as it was going to take.

Suddenly every nook and cranny of Sunnybank seemed to threaten her. She put her head down and walked fast. Away from where the blue lights flashed and the curtains twitched. She strode out and concentrated on the pavement. All that mattered was getting to the flat and locking the door and sliding home the chain and drawing the curtains and lifting the floor board under the mat in the back bedroom.

Sanctuary. Peace. Stillness like an Arctic lake. Ten million acres of cotton wool. And the flashing lights and the armies of bad memories could all stay outside in the street. Gone. Forgotten.

She counted steps. She avoided cracks. She barely checked for traffic when she crossed roads. And as she walked to safety she was watched by the bland screens of the gently moving CCTV cameras. And she was far too focused on escape to notice the young woman with the pushchair who was a hundred yards behind her all the way to the edge of Sunnybank. Then there was bearded student type with a red Kagool and an Ipod. Then there was a woman dressed like a bank manager with carefully done hair who was talking fast into a mobile phone. Last was a man in the uniform of one of the electricity companies with a clipboard and a pen.

They were all incidental. Bit part players. Background. Unimportant. Because her focus was all about a loose floorboard and a ticket to the greatest peace of all.

Two days later she donned sunglasses and a baseball cap and headed out to fill carrier bags for the freezer. She was planning on stocking up for a long hide. She would be self-sufficient whilst the storm raged outside. She would allow the time to drift and in the end everything would be fine. She had weeks worth of heroin and a place to hide from all the nightmares.

And then a police car had pulled up and a warrant for a breach of community service was served. And instead of returning to her sanctuary she was duly delivered to Loreburne Street police station.

How long now? Three times forever. Must be about lunchtime. Soon another tray would be passed through the door. That was a laugh. There was more chance of her running six marathons back-to-back than eating. The best thing about the trays was that they marked the passage of time. They proved that the clock hadn't stopped after all. There would be another at dinner time. Then three the next day. Then one for Monday morning. Then the Sheriff. Then back to the flat. And the floor board. And all the nightmares could be washed away . . ..

The door was cracking open. A good sign. The tray was here already. Time had actually gone quicker than she had realised. But there was no tray. Instead there were two of them in plain clothes. A few more questions Michelle. Interview room. A tape player. A few posters about nothing much on the wall. Her on one side of the table. Them the other. Somehow she knew she had to try and sit up and focus on a spot on the wall behind them. One of the posters. Maybe the one about thinking before drinking before driving. That was what Tony had said. She was sure it was. Find a spot on the wall and stare it down. But it wasn't all that easy when there were about a million maggots crawling up the inside of your legs and eating their way through your stomach whilst an army of poison dwarfs were pounding away at your bones with rubber hammers. The move from the cell had brought on nausea and she lurched off her seat to throw up in the plastic litter bin in the corner of the room. They waited patiently for her to finish and then nudged a glass of water toward her. One offered a cigarette and she took it with shaking hands and it was all that she could do to get the thing up to her lips and take a draw.

There were voices, but she could only really catch snatches of what they were saying. Something about a search warrant. Something about the stash. Something about her looking at five years. Something about it being a good idea for her to consider her options. Maybe if she were able to give them some details about Donald Dennison . . ..

And the walls closed in until the world became a great raging nightmare of sickness and despair.

Later now.

Days later.

Another cell. Prison this time. On remand. Already the word had been passed. Orders from the big man. One word and she was dead. One lousy word and she was history. Double D's word had been duly delivered and she had accepted it with eyes left vacant by days of pain. And still the agony showed no signs of letting go. Day three had been worse than anything she had ever imagined. And day four had been no better. Now it was day five and still it went on and on. No sleep. No let up. No relief. Pure unyielding torture. And alongside the pain were the memories. All over her now. Screaming at her from inches away from her ears.

She had two cell mates. One was a girl she knew vaguely. A Double D customer with cropped hair and arms coated in tattoos and teeth rotted by years of methadone. She had been the one who had passed the word. She had pulled a home made blade out from the back of her tracksuit bottoms and laid it on Chelle's cheek an inch under her eye. One word. One word and she would do the slicing. Because Double D appreciated those who looked after his interests. So. One word. Later the girl had cooked up on a piece of foil and leered at Chelle as she chased the dragon.

Her other cell mate was a young black woman who seemed completely unaware that there was anyone with her in the cell. She sat on her bunk and read a fat paperback with total focus. All day she never uttered a word. Only when the smoke licked up from the foil did her dark eyes lift up from the page to register bored disgust.

Chelle was a ball of pain. She clamped her eyes shut to try and force the agony from her body, but it only made it worse. The hours eased by and the sounds of the prison slowly faded and died into silence. Both cell mates fell to sleep leaving her all alone with her pain. She had seen where the knife had been hidden under the mattress.

All she had to do was to stand up quietly and reach out. It was the work of seconds. Then what? Then she could escape.

Two wrists. Cut, cut. A few moments of pain, but it would be no worse than the pain that was already in every molecule of her body. Then peace. Fade to black. No more pain. No more memories. No more guilt. No more regrets. No more nothing. Just long black silence.

Once the thought was in her head it was irresistible. A way out. It was all she wanted. Why the hell not? Her mind was razor sharp with the pain and her mind weighed up the situation and gave an answer. A simple answer that could not be argued with.

Nothing to live for.

Living only meant more pain. And more guilt. And more memories. And hundreds more nights in a cell before eventual release to a lifetime of loneliness. Life had become pain. Death would become peace. Easy choice.

She eased herself to her feet and gently pulled the blade out from under the mattress before sitting back on her bunk and exposing her wrists.

It was time.

"Why you do this?"

For a moment she was convinced that she was hearing voices, then she saw the bright eyes of the African woman fixed on her.

"Please. Just leave me alone. It's none of your business."

"So. Why you do this?"

"You wouldn't understand."

She heard a sucking of teeth. "You have pain I think. I know pain. I know too much pain. But I not making with knife. Why you do this? What about your mummy? Your daddy? Family? What they say? How they feel?"

"They won't care."

"They care."

"Look. Just leave me alone. I haven't seen them in years. They don't know me. I don't know them. It doesn't matter."

"They alive?"

"Yes. They're alive."

"Then you are lucky."

This made Chelle snort with laughter. Lucky? What was the stupid cow on about. Had she no idea?

"Oh yeah right. Lucky. I'm rattling my head off and staring down the barrel of five years unless I cut a deal then I'll probably get my face slashed up. So right. Dead lucky. That's me. Now why don't you shut up and leave me be."

"You have family. So you lucky."

"OK. Fine. Let's agree to that. I have family. Lucky me. Now please, just go back to sleep."

"You can see this family. Make phone call. Talk. It is good this way."

"I don't see how any of this is your business. If you want to talk to family, talk to your own and leave me be."

"It is not possible. My husband he was MDC. You know this?"

"Of course not."

"It is Zimbabwe. MDC. Movement for Democratic Change. They are people who try to remove Mugabe. One night, the soldiers they come. My husband, they kill him. My father, they kill him. My mother, they kill her. My little boy, they kill him. They kill with machete. Big knife. Everywhere he is blood. Me, maybe I am lucky. They rape me and leave me. So I come to Britain to find safe. I take a boat from Belfast. They stop me and say I need papers. I say give me safe. Give me how you say Asylum. They say too late. I need to ask this thing in Ireland. So they bring me here. They say I can stay here under these terrorist law. Maybe they send me home now? Maybe I not to much lucky. So you can make this call I think."

The great eyes seemed to swallow her and soon her own eyes were swimming with tears.

"Is that true?"

"Is true. All true. You can give me this knife I think."

Chelle passed the knife. Except she didn't. Because it was Michelle that passed the knife. "Your name?"

"My name is Selina. Your name?"

"Michelle. I am Michelle."

The next day Michelle made the call and three days later her mum and dad waited for her in the visiting hall. By this stage the pain had all but completely passed. All her barriers were down, laid out on the ground like the aftermath of a street riot. Sleep was a complete impossibility, but her nights were no longer an eternity of empty space. Now her nights were filled with the quiet melodic voice of Selina. Two young women from opposite corners of the planet shared their pain. Michelle unpacked the suitcases that had gathered dust for years at the back of the cupboard and once all of the guilt was laid out on the table, it didn't seem so bad any more. She had done bad things, but they were nothing when compared to smashing into a family home and slaughtering a family with a machete. Selina told her all about a country that had once been beautiful. The bread basket of Africa. A place where big fat corn cobs would be harvested in abundance every year. And she told of how her homeland had become a giant prison. A killing field where the harvest was no longer corn. Selina drained the poison out of Michelle. Now it seemed that to yearn for the escape of heroin seemed to be an ultimate cowardice. If Selina could still find the heart to fight, then so could she.

For five minutes she was unable to speak with her parents. All the pent up emotion inside her burst in a flood of tears and all she could do was to hang on to them and cry. At last when she released them, her dad told her that he had been to see the family solicitor and everything was not as bad as it seemed. Of course Michelle had been staying at a flat where there had been a massive quantity of heroin, but the police had no evidence that she was actually selling it. He said that he had cashed in some savings and there was a barrister that the solicitor had recommended from Glasgow who had a fine reputation. Everyone was confident that the charges could be reduced to possession.

Michelle smiled.

"It's OK dad. Really. I'm not lying any more. I've done my lying for a lifetime. I'll plead guilty."

They had argued, but there was something in her eyes that told them that it was pointless. Her mum pulled a pile of bumpf from her bag. She explained that she had been to a place in town where they had told her what options there were. There were rehab clinics. There was help waiting when she was back out. There was hope by the bucket.

And Michelle carried on smiling, overwhelmed by the fact that the love had not died. When her mother had finished running through the pile of leaflets Michelle spoke in a strangely calm voice.

"A few nights ago I was about to kill myself. There was nowhere left to go. I had come to the end."

Her mum was about to speak, her eyes wide in horror, but Michelle gently demanded silence with a wave of a thin white hand.

" . . . My cell mate saved my life. Selina. She showed me there was still hope. She showed that there is always hope, no matter how bad things seem."

As youngsters raced around the visiting area with crisps and cartons of juice, Michelle told her parents the story of the young African woman who had watched her whole family being butchered before being subjected to multiple rape. She told the story of the young woman's two-year journey from the low hills of Matabeleland to HMP Dumfries. She explained how they were keeping her locked up using the new Anti Terror laws, how they were using the time to get the papers filled in to put Selina back on a plane to Harare. Maybe her parents would be willing to use some of the money to fight for Selina's life? An exchange for saving the life of their daughter. She explained how having an address was important. If Selina could use their home as an address, then she might be released and able to fight her asylum claim. Maybe she could use Michelle's old room? Maybe she could learn to ride the horses?

It was about a life for a life.

It was about hope in exchange for hope.

Three weeks later Selina stood in a bedroom that had once been the domain of a sixteen-year-old girl who had never dreamed that she was about to walk the dark road. Same posters on the wall. Same CD collection. Same rosettes from riding competition at country shows.

Every day she wrote long letters to the prison.

And every day she received a long letter in return.

And eighteen months later she was there to meet her friend when she was released. She took along her new British passport to prove that miracles really could happen.

And the friend that she met was called Michelle.

Order Form

Name ----------------------------------

Address ----------------------------------

Telephone ----------------------------------

Email ----------------------------------

Please send me ----------------- **Copies of**

'Roads to Down'

Return this form to:

Glenmill Publishing
Glenmill
Dumfries
DG2 8PX

Or Telephone   01387 270861